Ayad

....

Frank Lloyd

Contents

Chapter 1

"Aye! Aye! Aye! Get it!" The ladies voice yelled over the loud music. The night club was packed out and the drinks kept coming. The group was on a girls trip to Florida, and after weeks of bickering over trip details and saving up, the time to let loose had finally arrived.

There was never a shortage of pretty girls in Miami nightclubs, but Gracie and her friend group stood out that night. They were turning every head. Gracie noticed Becca staring at a guy from across the room. "Who's catching your eye?" Gracie loudly asked, barely able to even hear herself.

"Girl, I think he's coming." Becca flipped her long tresses over the shoulder and poker faced.

A gentleman approached the group, with two men in black following close behind him. He was average height, Arab, and strikingly handsome. From head to toe it was strictly designer. His light green eyes were fixed on Gracie as he spoke, "You lot had something to drink?"

His faint British accent caught the girls off guard. Leni pretended to fan her face, "Are you asking to buy us all a drink, baby?"

"Get whatever you want, it's on me!" He flashed a pearly white smile at Gracie again.

"He got money, money!" Leni cackled while bee-lining to the bar, with Becca and others following behind.

Gracie didn't go. She continued to sit in her spot with the gentleman now walking over and sitting next to her. "I'm Saheed, what's your name pretty?"

"Graciella. I go by Gracie." She shyly looked away, his gaze on her was intense.

"You don't want anything to drink?"

"I don't drink." She said flatly, she never had a taste for alcohol or drugs and intended to keep it that way.

"Come on, just one. I'm paying for it!" He moved closer to her, the smell of his cologne filling her lungs.

"I guess you'll have to buy me something else then." Gracie raised an eyebrow, now having fun with the playful flirting.

Saheed grabbed her hand, "My dad's a billionaire, I'll buy you anything you want"

-

And buy Gracie anything she wanted, Saheed did. He took her on lavish shopping trips, the nicest restaurants and it all led up to the 3 carat engagement ring on her finger roughly 8 months of long-distance dating after that night in the club.

The pair had just finished up a nightmare date where they couldn't stop arguing throughout. Saheed's driver silently put the car in park in front of

Gracie's house. Before he could come around the car to open the door for her, she opened it herself and walked quickly towards the front door.

Saheed rushed out the car, following behind. "Gracie! Gracie!"

She spun around and glared at him. "What?"

"Why are you fussing about? I'm a man, Gracie! You can't possibly expect me to not have needs."

"That's not the issue, Saheed. The issue is you aren't letting this entire matter rest. I have been open to you since day one that I am waiting until marriage. It was never a secret. It's a strong conviction of mine and you told me that you could wait." Gracie crossed her arms over her chest. "I don't want to keep fighting with you about this. You either accept it or we call it good."

"Thought relationships were about compromise?"

"Goodnight, Saheed."

"Wait, wait, wait!" He grabbed her arm to stop her from going inside the house. "I'll leave it. If you want to wait, that's fine."

"Are you just saying that?"

"It will be challenging, look at you." He took a step back and smiled at Gracie. She had deep brown skin, a petite frame, full pink lips, high cheekbones, and beautiful long hair. There wasn't a magazine she could not grace with her feminine charm. "Look at my lady!"

"Stop." Gracie let out a small laugh and playfully hit Saheed's chest. "You play too much."

"I can't wait to bring you back to my mum and dad. You will love them."

"Gosh, I hope they love me." She shifted from side to side, and looked out into the night sky. "This whole thing is really... different for me. I've never lived with a guy before, talkless of his entire family, you know?"

"Just chill on it. My family is proper laid back, well, maybe not my brother, Dabir is all stuffy, all business...blah, blah, blah."

Gracie felt nervous. Saheed always described his brother as being overly serious and a killjoy. He was much more concerned with carrying on the family legacy than Saheed was. Dabir was in and out of meetings, constantly, he was the Managing Director for his dad's media conglomerate, AES.

Saheed on the other hand, took whatever cut he got in his allowances and splurged it all on choice liquor, designer clothes, luxury cars and trips. Saheed would tell Gracie about how unenjoyable Dabir was to be around, it made her feel nervous every time she thought of the move.

"I hope it all goes well with him, it's just one more week until we all live together." Gracie took a deep breath, and then put her arms around Saheed in an embrace. "I have to go get ready for bed, I have work in the morning."

"Ah come on, girl, no! Just quit, you know I can provide for you."

She gave him a kiss on the cheeks. "Good night."

Chapter 2

G racie was off from work, packing up the last luggage filled with clothes. It was surreal that she was preparing to move into the house of her future in-laws. In their family line, it has always been the expectation for son's to bring their fiancée to live with the family for a year. While separate bedrooms are required, the year is designed to give the couple space to see if a lifetime together is a good fit for themselves and for the family. Every married person had completed that requirement in the past 125 years, and the couples are sometimes even invited to live at the familial house after marriage.

Thankfully, Gracie did not have to pack alone and be stuck in her own thoughts. She had her closest friend Becca and Leni there to keep her company. Leni picked up a pair of Gracie's Louboutin heels. "Now that you're off the streets, you won't need these no' more. Can I have 'em?"

Gracie nodded a yes, before she could talk, Becca interjected. "Len, you 'finna break your legs squeezing into those shoes."

"What are you talking about? I'm only a size 10."

"My point exactly! Gracie is a 5."

Leni thought about it for a second, but the shoes ultimately were too cute for her to ignore. She sat on the floor and braced to squeeze her foot into the slender heel. "Where there is a will there's a way!"

Leni wobbily stood up to prove her point, but before she could straighten up, she went crashing down on the floor. Gracie and Becca burst out laughing at the sight. Becca covered her mouth while cackling.

She said, "B****, that was giving Cinderella's step sisters in that glass shoe!"

Leni rolled her eyes and tried not to laugh at herself, "Whatever, y'all can keep those baby shoes. My birthday is rolling around the corner, and I expect some of the Arab money you got to come my way."

Gracie was still laughing, when suddenly the bedroom door swung up and her sleepy mom scowled with arms crossed. Becca, Leni and Gracie all stopped laughing. In her thick Nigerian accent, Gracie's mom asked "Do you know the hour it is? What's the noise about?!"

Becca and Leni smiled tight lipped. They had been friends with Gracie since elementary so Gracie's mom was also like their own mom. Gracie smiled at her mom, "Sorry mommy, we were just goofing off. We will be done here soon."

"You aren't small girls anymore, how can you be laughing like an animal at this time? Is that how you girls will behave in your husbands house? He will make you pack out!"

Leni smirked mischievously and then sat back against the bed frame, "I have a few tricks up my sleeve. Whenever I do get married, that man is going to be hooked." She looked at Gracie and winked.

"Ahh, is that so? You think marriage is only about the bedroom, abi? Bad girl." Gracie's mom lifted her hand and pretended she was going to hit

Leni. There was now a smile on her face as well. Deep down, she loved Gracie's friends. Except for one of them.

"Sorry I'm late y'all!" A voice called from downstairs. "I'm coming up!"

Gracie's mom rolled her eyes and in a low voice said, "Don't say too much to that girl ooo, she doesn't need to know about your private affairs."

"Ah ah, mommy. Why do you dislike her so much?"

"I've already told you! She's not your friend." Gracie's mom looked to her side and Alexis was now approaching.

"Hey girl, how are you?"

"I'm not your girl, and go take off your shoes, I don't have a maid." Gracie's mom frowned and then turned to go back into her bedroom.

Alexis kicked off her Stiletto's and walked in the bedroom. She was a classic Southern beauty, and she made a killing with it. Alexis turned heads everywhere she went. "Sorry I'm late y'all. Doc held me up."

"You're still with that married man?" Becca asked.

"Uh, no. He's still with me." Alexis smirked while looking in the mirror at her reflection. "They're just checks, darling, sorry to their wives for marrying weak willed men."

"Here we go with this again." Leni grumbled, rolling her eyes.

The air of the room always felt different when Alexis was there. As kids, they all were carefree and goofy, but as time progressed, Alexis slightly drifted from the group due to the pretentious attitude she developed with time.

Becca and Leni couldn't stand her, Gracie on the other hand, was deeply loyal to her friends and continued to hold on.

"So fill me in babe, tomorrow is the big day!" Alexis briefly looked away from the mirror and to Gracie who was almost done folding.

"Tomorrow is the big day, it's all so crazy to me." Gracie reached for her makeup bag. "He is sending his guys over tomorrow morning to get all the stuff."

"So, what is it like a trial marriage? They wanna' make sure sonnie boy's wife can cook and clean and ****?"

"Lex, come on now, don't be gross." Gracie pleaded. "Well, I guess that's kinda what I thought at first actually too. I thought it was going to be some weird housewife test, but they have multiple cooks and maids. It's just a standing family tradition."

"Just mom and dad?"

"No, he has a sister too actually, her name is Sarai. Then there's the oldest, Dabir. But Saheed said I probably won't see either around too much. I guess he works a lot and the sister is in med school. But Saheed thinks I'll probably have the hardest time impressing him out of everyone else."

"Have sex with his dad, then nothing the older brother says will even matter." Alexis shrugged, "That's at least what I would do."

Gracie looked at Alexis with an eyebrow raised, "Yeah, no. That's not happening. Not in a million years."

"Anyways." Becca side eyed Alexis, she was starting to get tired of Alexis being around the group. She wondered why Gracie continued bringing her around. She held one of Gracie's hands. "Babe, it's you. It's impossible not to love you, you'll do just fine this year. I already know by this time next year we are going to be dancing it up at your wedding. Don't stress."

Gracie squeezed Becca's hand and smiled warmly. Leni gave her a playful shove. "Yeah girl, don't even trip. If anyone deserves to marry into a great family, it's you. And if they do you wrong, may God handle them accordingly."

"Amen!" Becca yelled as Gracie pulled them into a hug and the three embraced on the ground. Alexis stood over them and smiled through tight lips.

Chapter 3

T he next morning was busy. Before Gracie could even get out of the shower, Saheed's guys were downstairs moving the luggage out the house. After her shower, Gracie hurriedly got dressed in a pair of leggings and a knit dress. She put her hair into a sleek, high ponytail and put on a layer of shiny lip gloss on her pink lips.

Graie's mom watched the men move about from a distance. When Gracie caught eye contact with her mom, she saw the sadness in her eyes. "Mommy, please no. You'll make me cry."

""I'm not crying." She looked the other way. "Omo mi, wa."

Gracie met her mom and the two held each other in a tight embrace. Gracie's mom pulled out of the hug so she could hold Gracie's face. "Ife mi, my spirit doesn't like this boy, are you sure this is what you want?"

She somberly nodded.

"Okay, if it's what you want, I will support you. Just don't forget the daughter of who you are. Love is not by force ooo, if he beats you. Are you listening? If he beats you, come back home chap chap. No one will blame you, okay?"

"Okay! Okay!" Gracie laughed, "I'll call you tonight when I get settled."

"Okay ooo, safe journeys."

Gracie put on a big smile for her mom and held tightly to the purse on her shoulder. Gracie used all the strength she had to remain composed in front of her mom, but the second she was hidden behind the ultra tinted car windows, she broke down in tears from the pain of telling her mom goodbye for the first time.

Little did she know, inside the house, her mother was doing the same.

-

A long drive later, Gracie gently woke up from her broken heart induced sleep in the back of the car. They were pulling up into a long, password protected property with a driveway lined with trim, green hedges. At the end of the driveway there was a large fountain with water spouting out of it and gracefully dropping back in. There were multiple luxury cars lining the driveway, some Gracie was able to recognize as Saheed's.

The house itself was magnificent from the outside, it was a large Spanish villa inspired mansion with artistically placed arches and windows all around. Gracie stood still and took it all in. She knew that Saheed was of an affluent background, but standing there in that moment put it into further perspective.

As she beheld the house, Saheed excitedly dashed out the house. "About time!"

Gracie ran over to him and hugged him tightly. It was the beginning of a new chapter for their relationship, and Gracie was overdone with excitement. "This is crazy!"

"It feels very much like a dream for me. Come in, so I can introduce you to the 'fam.'"

Hand in hand, the pair entered the house. At the front door Gracie stopped to take off the knee high boots she was wearing, but Saheed quickly stopped her. "Babe, don't worry 'bout that. No one cares."

"Oh, no, that's okay. I'm used to taking my shoes off indoors. I don't want to track around water from the rain."

"We have a maid, just keep it on!" Saheed snapped with irritability, "Your fit won't look right without it."

"Is this something really worth getting angry over?"

"Well you tell me! Is this whole shoes thing worth ticking me off? Take. Off. Your. Shoes."

"Saheed!" A woman called out, appalled. A young woman with striking green eyes and dark long hair walked over with a frown. "Not everyone is like you, and insist on wearing shoes everywhere. Why are you fussing?"

Saheed rolled his eyes and looked the other way. The woman looked at Gracie and stretched out her arms for a hug. "I'm Sarai, his sister."

"Little sister! I'm still older."

Gracie hugged her back, "Hi, Sarai. It's so nice to meet you, he's talked quite a bit about you. Med school, right?"

"Yup! At this point I might as well just be a professional student." She flashed a smile out, "My parents and brother are in the other room, let me take you over."

"Dabir is home?" Saheed asked nervously.

"Yeah, he had a meeting nearby and stopped home to talk with dad about something. You know how he is." Sarai smiled, "He has a little bit of a cold exterior, but you will love him, Gracie. Dabir is a total sweetheart."

"Sweetheart? He's the devil, you stay away from him Gracie." Saheed urged while grabbing tightly to Gracie's hand.

The pair continued walking down the long marbled hallway until they arrived into a foyer/sitting area that was ornately decorated with golden fixtures and accents, and a brightly colored Turkish rug covering the floor. There sat a middle aged couple dressed in traditional clothing.

Gracie put on the most charming smile she could muster as she graciously waved at the two, "It's so very nice to finally meet you, my name is—"

"Gracie, sit, please." The man nodded towards the chair that was adjacent to where he sat. Gracie quickly obliged, and Saheed joined her in the next spot. He looked between Gracie and Saheed. "Welcome to our home. We have been expecting you.

"Thank you for having me, it's absolutely beautiful, just gorgeous."

"That credit goes to my darling wife, Mrs. Ayad." He turned to his wife who sat next to him and she shyly smiled.

Mrs. Ayad looked at Gracie from head to toe. While she never pictured her son marrying a black girl, Gracie was beautiful and seemed to be polite. She was going to try her best to be open minded. But something about Gracie was familiar, "We've met, no? I have seen you somewhere."

"Oh, I don't..I don't think so. Maybe someone who looked like me?"

"Well, it's so nice to meet the girl my Saheed has decided to be his wife. Do you work? Are you in school?"

"I graduated with my Masters in Mental Counseling a few years back, I'm working as a therapist for a women's health clinic." Gracie brimmed, she loved what she did. Her main demographic was women getting therapy for postpartum depression, fertility issues and grief over child loss. Gracie felt joy about getting to help those women. It's absolutely amazing, the clinic offers medical care, massage therapy, lactation consultation, nutrition services, therapy and–"

"But she'll be quitting once we get married and all that. She'll be keeping you company at home, Umi." Saheed interjected, with a big grin. "Focus on them babies!"

Mr. and Mrs. Ayad laughed. Mr Ayad scooted forward in his seat, "We can't wait to have grandkids to fill this entire house!"

"Don't worry, Baba. By this time next year we will be working on #1!"

The trio laughed, and Gracie gave a courtesy one. She felt upset at the way Saheed had cut her off. A few more moments went by with them conversing, before Gracie got a tour of the home. At the end of the tour, they brought her into the room that she would be staying at for the next year. It was a large room with a four-poster bed with pale pink covers. It was connected to an en suite bathroom and walk -in closet.

Chapter 4

G racie spent most of that evening unpacking her clothes, but around 5, took a shower to get gussied up with dinner with the entire family. The shower head had multiple jets and was pristinely clean. She felt like a whole new person by the time she got out.

She slipped into a silk black dress and black heels. She curled her hair into loose body waves and was putting on makeup right as there were knocks on the door. Saheed opened the door, "Baby baby! Looking fine as per usual. Dabir is going to be proper jealous when he sees you."

She shook her head while putting on a matte, red lipstick. "Why are you always so strung up about Dabir? It seems like all he does is work. Where does he have time to be an issue for you?"

"Babe, please. You don't get it." He shook his head, "Why are you always defending him?"

"Defendi–Come on, Saheed. I'm not defending him, I was just asking." Gracie sprayed her face with a setting spray. "I just feel like you can be a bit on edge when it comes to him, but you've never told me why."

"You don't know!" He yelled.

"Woah, take it easy, I'm just trying to understand." Gracie walked over to Saheed and moved to touch his arm but he flinched it back. "Saheed, calm down, seriously."

"Alright, you're right." He pinched the bridge of his nose and put a hand on his hip, "Let's go. The car is waiting."

In a cutting silence, the pair left the bedroom and walked out front to the black Lamborgini out front. In celebration of Gracie moving in that night, Mr. Ayad rented out a restaurant downtown for family and close friends to enjoy.

From the point they got there, it was like Saheed turned his normal personality back on. He was incredibly sociable and charismatic as he introduced Gracie to the guests that were there.

A staff was on rotation handing out hor dourves and choice drinks. Mr. Ayad came behind Gracie and tapped her on the shoulder. She spun around and was relieved to see a somewhat familiar face. "Oh, hello!"

"Are you enjoying yourself?"

"Yes! I am at a loss for words with all of this, thank you again for welcoming me into the family. This is much more of a welcome than I ever could have imagined."

He grabbed her hand and gave it a squeeze, "Let me show you to some of our countries dignitaries."

The two began walking through the crowd of people, before Mr. Ayad stopped in his tracks, "Dabir!" He pulled Gracie behind him towards the entrance where a tall, well built man stood. His eyes were a much darker green than his siblings, and he stood heads taller than the whole family. He wore a suit that was simple, yet clearly expensive. His jaw was chiseled and defined, with a well trimmed beard covering it.

"My son." Mr. Ayad reached up and held Dabir's face in his hands. "I'm glad you're here today."

Dabir held an emotionless face despite his dad's affectionate gesture. He slightly bowed his head at his dad as Mr. Ayad let go of his face. Dabir then turned his eyes to a star-struck Gracie. She was finally meeting the much talked about Dabir. While there were minor facial similarities between the two, everything else about Dabir and Saheed were different. Dabir's mannerisms were composed and calm while Saheed was always moving about and had a tendency to be jittery.

"Gracie, meet Dabir."

The two locked eyes for a moment, Gracie feeling her breath getting caught in her throat. She played it off and broke eye contact, "It's nice to finally meet you, I've heard so much."

He reached out his hand to Gracie, when she took his hand in hers, he firmly gave it a shake. Gracie pulled her hand back and gave a polite smile, "I'm sure we will get to know each other more."

By this point he still had not spoken a word, he gave Gracie a slight smile.

Abruptly, Saheed rushed behind Gracie, wrapping his arms around her waist. She could smell alcohol on him. "Big bro! You met my fiancée! Isn't she hot?"

The little smile that was on Dabir's face was now gone as he sternly watched his little brother erratically move about, yelling as he spoke.. Mr. Ayad was abhorred, "Saheed!"

"What, Baba?" Saheed put both his hands up in surrender, "I did good! I'm the first son to get married, and will give you the first grand kids too!"

"It's not a competition, Saheed."

"Oh yeah right! You are proper jealous, just look at her!" Saheed roughly grabbed Gracie by the waist to show off her shape.

Gracie was horrified and pushed his hands away. "What are you doing?! Stop!"

Dabir spoke up, his voice deep and Arabic accent faint. "Yah! That's enough. It's enough."

In that moment, Gracie learned that what Dabir spoke had some heavy weight. All he did was give a look to some of the security guards across the room, and before anyone knew it, Saheed was swiftly and quietly ushered out.

Mr. Ayad begged Gracie to stay and enjoy her welcome party despite Saheed having to leave, but she felt it was wrong to do so. During the ride in the car, he went from grief to rage to blank, cyclically. "Baby, take it easy. You had too much to drink." Gracie smoothed her hand through Saheed's hair, she felt exhausted.

He pushed her hand back and then put his head in his hands. "What were you talking about with him?!"

"We— I mean, nothing really. Your dad was introducing us."

"Was he talking about me?!"

"What? No. Saheed, please just take it easy, okay? He barely even said two words" Gracie calmly urged, putting her hand on his chest. "Look at me, hey, look at me."

Saheed looked over with red eyes. Gracie walked him through a breathing exercise that she did with her clients. He was able to calm down, but the rest of the car ride was in silence. The silence was loud.

It was going to be a long year.

Chapter 5

B y the next morning, Gracie woke up feeling doubt in her heart about how the pre-marital year would go. She did not like what she was seeing of him, but wanted to give him the benefit of the doubt.

Gracie pushed the busy thoughts out of her head and focused on getting ready for work, since she would have to leave earlier to get there on time. It was around 5:30 AM when she left her bedroom to leave the house.

The house was quiet and still, as everyone was still asleep, or so Gracie thought. She rounded the corner to pass through the kitchen, and was filled with shock to see Dabir standing there. He turned and looked at her, he was wearing a fitted white button up that was neatly tucked into his dark blue dress pants.

"Good Morning! I was surprised to see anyone else up this early!" Gracie smiled widely, putting a hand on her heart. "I'm not going to lie, I was a bit startled."

"Morning." He put his attention back to his laptop.

"Eesh, looks like I'm not the only one starting the work day early." Gracie awkwardly joked, she had heard such bad things about Dabir, in that moment she felt as though she was on thin ice.

"At 5am?" He asked.

"Well, usually no, but I don't know how bad traffic is in this area. I figured it was best to head over early just in case, it's all the way in Greenleaf."

Dabir gave her a disapproving look. "It's morning, yet it's still dark out. I can drive you there."

"Oh! Oh, no, no, that won't be necessary. I can just take an uber or something, seriously it's fine.

"It's fine, let's go." He shut his laptop. "We will arrange for you to have your own driver from tomorrow on.

"Oh, gosh that's a lot, well and thank you. You don't have the drivers take you around?"

"I have my own car and my own hands." He responded plainly, walking past her towards the front door. "Let's go."

Gracie hurried behind him, and was led to a simple, sleek Mercedes that was parked up front. Dabir opened the door for Gracie and waited for her to get her seatbelt on and settled before shutting the door and crossing over to his side..

Gracie noticed how he drove with one hand on the steering wheel and the other leaned against the door, she could tell there was a lot on his mind.

Perhaps it was the heart of a therapist in her, but she found herself feeling empathy for Dabir. She knew first hand that Saheed made no contributions to the family business, everything was on Dabir's plate.

"Do you usually start your work day at 5?"

"Why?"

"I'm just curious, everyone else in there was asleep...Saheed always talks about how hard you work."

He glanced over at Gracie then back to the road, "They said you work at a women's clinic, yeah?"

"Yeah, I'm a therapist! Been doing it for a few years."

"That's good." He replied, "People need it."

"Thank you." A small smile spread on Gracie's face, for this was the first person in the entire family to finally acknowledge Gracie's career. Dabir did not say much, but it still meant a lot to Gracie. Perhaps the bar was low, but she still felt affirmed. "Saheed said you work at your dad's company, what do you do there?"

"Everything."

"Such as...? Like, do you help in marketing? PR? Sales?..."

"I'm an accountant by trade." He started, but then paused to listen to the GPS. "I joined the company as the Director of Finance, but as my father got older I was named Managing Director of Operations."

"Sounds like a lot, do you like it?"

"Sometimes, there are things more important than whether you like it or not..."

To Gracie's surprise, Dabir was talking to her. Saheed mentioned how horrible and cold Dabir was, but Gracie wasn't picking up on any of that. Yeah, he was on the quiet end but by no means do

The rest of the ride went on in a peaceful, comfortable silence. Too comfortable, as Gracie dozed off in sleep.

"Hey...Hey, you're here." Dabir called out, in his deep, calm voice. When Gracie didn't respond he gently nudged her shoulder. She woke up in surprise. "You're here."

"Oh my gosh, sorry." She sat up, looking away in embarrassment. She looked outside the window and saw that they were pulled up in front of her work place. "I didn't realize that I was so tired...But, thank you for dropping me off, that was really kind of you, Dabir.

"It's no problem."

A small smile spread on her face, "Have a good day at work."

She exited the car and smoothed her hands over the emerald green body con she was wearing. Her long hair blew in the wind as she waved Dabir good bye and went up the stairs into the clinic she worked in.

"That's the fiancée? He's hot." The middle aged security guard said as she squinted at Dabir's car, trying to take in his image as much as she could.

"Oh, gosh, Rhonda, no. That's his brother." Gracie responded as she put down her purse, so she could pass through the metal detector. The facility was heavily secured and a part of it being a safe space, meant everyone had to be checked for recording devices and weapons.

"His brother? Damn! He single? I don't mind being your sister-in-law."

Gracie laughed, "I actually do think he's single, he's quite sweet too. If I find out he's looking, you'll be the first person I recommend, yeah?"

"My girl!" Rhonda winked, laughing out loud. "I'm getting tired of working girl. I need me a rich son too."

Gracie took her purse on the other side and in high spirits went into her office. She didn't know why, but she felt like she could conquer the world that day. She saw five clients for 60-minute sessions, ran a group therapy on PPD, and then squeezed in one last intake assessment before she threw in the towel and packed her bag to go home.

She said her goodbye to all the practitioners who were still at the clinic and made her way out the front door. She figured she would have to get a ride-share back home, but to her surprise, there was a car waiting for her up front. A smile spread on her face, and she pulled out her phone to call Saheed as she walked.

"Hey!" Saheed answered in a chipper voice, music blaring in the background.

"Hey, we didn't talk all day. How are you?"

"I'm just out with some of my boys, where have you been? The help said they didn't see you leave when I asked."

"Uhh, I was at work."

"Work? Why didn't you quit yet? You literally don't have to anymore, G."

Gracie opened her mouth to respond but then paused, she didn't know what to say. She took a deep breath and let it out, choosing peace in that moment. "Well, I was just calling to thank you for sending a car over, uber's can creep me out sometimes."

"My drivers are with me, I don't know what you're on about."

"But..." Gracie paused before opening the door. She walked around to the drivers side and clearly recognized the car as one she frequently saw parked at the house. She put the phone to her shoulder and knocked on the window for him to wind down.

"Miss. Gracie." He rushed out the car to open the door for her.

She didn't take a step toward the door. "Did Mr. Ayad send you?"

"No madam, I was sent by Sir. Dabir. He told me I am to take you to work and bring you home from now on."

Her mouth widened in shock. "Oh, okay. I—um, I didn't know that. But thank you." She smiled at the man and stepped in the car. She put the phone back to her ear to update Saheed but by that point he had already hung up.

She rolled her eyes as she put on her seat belt, his attitude could be so finicky and she was not a fan of it at times. Gracie looked over at the older man, with thin gray hair in a ponytail. He had a cheery countenance and stocky build. "I didn't catch your name."

"Hakeem." He grinned. "When we park I will give you my contact information, anywhere you need to go, any time, just call."

"How will you have time to drive me and others?"

"No others, he hired me just for you."

Gracie was speechless. It was a weird chapter of her life, but one thing she knew for sure, was Dabir was not as bad as he was being made out to be.

Chapter 6

The next day was a Friday. Gracie woke up full of excitement, it was a Friday and Gracie had the day off, she wanted to finally carve out some time to get started on some wedding planning.

And what better way to do it than with her best friends? She was planning to have them over in the afternoon for brunch out in the outdoor cabana and some light-hearted wedding chat. Gracie got dressed in her cutest, beige, sweat suit and put her long hair into a bun on the top of her head. She hurried downstairs to start on some food for her friends and herself. In the kitchen she saw Mrs. Ayad drinking tea.

Mrs. Ayad looked Gracie up and down, she was still trying to get a read on her. On the other end, Gracie was doing the same. She didn't sense the same warmth that she typically got from Mr. Ayad. "Good Morning, how was your night?" The two hugged.

"Oh it was nice. No work today?" Mrs. Ayad always spoke slowly and calculatedly. The words rolled off her tongue like a knife going through butter. Smooth and precise.

"I don't work Fridays, usually just Monday through Thursday. The option is there, but I just find that I feel better if I have one extra day to my weekend" She leaned against the marble counter. "Oh! I am having some friends over today to help with wedding planning. I don't know if you are free or not but I'd love for you to join us for a bit. Saheed did mention that you would probably want us to do a more traditional wedding."

A smile spread on her face. "Just let me know when and I will be there. Why don't you have Raamatu prepare some food for your guests?"

"That's okay, I was planning on cooking, I don't mind it at all."

"Darling." She placed a hand on Gracie's shoulder. "If you want to be an Ayad, you need to start living like an Ayad. The help cooks."

Gracie and Mrs. Ayad stood there in silence, eye-to-eye. In that moment Gracie realized that she didn't like Mrs. Ayad and it seemed that the sentiment was mutual from Mrs. Ayad to Gracie. Mrs. Ayad gracefully put down her teacup, turned towards the hallway and began to yell for the staff. Gracie couldn't understand Arabic, anyone could tell that Mrs. Ayad was speaking harshly and condescending.

Raamatu, the head cook, ran into the kitchen flustered. She began to pull ingredients from the fridge and robotically dicing vegetables. Gracie gave a small yet uncomfortable smile to her future mother-in-law before leaving the room. The encounter didn't sit right, Gracie mentally questioned what kind of family she had gotten herself involved with.

Especially since Gracie's mother used to be a cook for a rich family. When she was pregnant with Gracie, she worked as a nanny for a wealthy family. She shared with Gracie the horrors of the family's treatment towards her. That alone encouraged Gracie to treat everyone well always, regardless of status, wealth or supposed glory.

Within the hour, Gracie was outside with Leni, Becca and Alexis enjoying the ridiculously elaborate breakfast spread of shakshuka, various fruits, fresh flat breads and more.

Leni took a big bite of her food and washed it down with fresh orange juice, "Girl, you have GOT to be kidding me! You're living like this now?!"

Gracie shrugged her shoulders, she saw the appeal to the glitz and glamor of it all, but she still was ruminating over the way Mrs. Ayad yelled at Raamatu. Gracie couldn't get the fearful look on Raamatu's face, out of her mind. The memory was turning her off the lifestyle. "I'm trying to get used to it."

"I could get used to it." Alexis snapped her fingers. "Just like that. Be sharp mama, there's probably a wait list of girls gunning for your place."

Becca rolled her eyes, she couldn't stand Alexis. She looked back to Gracie, "What's meant to be, will be. Don't let the money trick you, YOU are the catch here, not him."

"Look how rich he is! And you're saying he's not the catch?!" Alexis scoffed.

"Alright y'all, nothing to be alarmed at, it's just Alexis being Alexis." Leni sarcastically announced. "Same story, different day."

"You guys, I thought this was supposed to be wedding planning, what's all this?" Gracie questioned. "Come on, I only have a year."

"And NO budget!" Saheed announced, stepping outside just in time to hear only what Gracie said. "How's my lady doing? Hope you are all doing alright!"

Saheed wrapped his arms around the seated Gracie. He gave her a big kiss on the side of her head. Alexis stood to her feet and stretched out a dainty hand towards him, "We've heard nothing but good things. I'm Alexis, so happy to finally meet the man who has made my best friend so happy."

Becca and Leni shot each other a look.

Saheed grabbed her hands and froze, "Wait... Alexis...Alexis Malone?"

"In the flesh!" She smiled widely and gave Saheed the eyes. She loved when men recognized her from her social media pages, she loved it even more when the men were rich. "You follow me?"

"Ah, well, I–uh, no." His eyes nervously darted between Gracie and Alexis. "I think I–uh, saw a post on the explore page or something."

"Well, I'm glad we could meet." Alexis slowly tilted over to pick up her handbag. "I actually do have some appointments to get to, can you show me out? I don't want to get lost in your mansion."

"What? Girl, you just got here!" Gracie protested.

"I know, I'm sorry babes. But you know how busy I can be!" She blew a kiss to Gracie, "But you girls enjoy it."

"Right this way." Saheed grinned, walking her out.

The trio went on with their own discussion, with plenty of laughing and joking throughout. They spent a few hours enjoying each other's company, before evening rolled around and they went home. Gracie was in the main living room, watching tv and trying Saheed's phone. He wasn't one to be home early, ever, but it seemed odd to Gracie that he wasn't at least answering.

To make matters worse, Saheed's parents were out of the house for an event as well.

It felt like she was in the

Getting tired of waiting, she decided to indulge in a sweet treat. She was baking some brownies in the kitchen by herself, and listening to music.

Lost in the music, Gracie didn't notice Dabir walk in, breezing past the kitchen with tunnel vision. When Gracie looked up and saw him move in the corner of her eye, she flinched and took an EarPod out of her ear.

"Gosh, you scared me! What has you in such a rush? Moving around like a spirit" Gracie teased.

He let out a small chuckle and ran a hand through his wavy hair, he was also so focused that he didn't see Gracie. "I did not see you, sorry."

"That's okay, I know you're always busy." She pointed at the bar stool across the kitchen island. "Have a seat, I'm making brownies and they are almost ready."

"Brownies? Some kind of cake or something?"

"Yeah! Well...sort of. You haven't had brownies before?"

"No. I don't think so."

"You have to try some, come on, sit sit sit."

Dabir obliged. He sat on the bar stool and sighed as if it was his first time sitting all day. He loosened the tie from his neck and took off his suit jacket. Gracie caught the sight of him doing this in the corner of her eye, he was dangerously handsome. As her face heated up, she diverted her attention back to the brownies.

As she carried the hot pan out the oven using a kitchen towel, Raamatu happened to be passing by and freaked out. She hurried over to take it out of Gracie's hands but Gracie resisted. "It's okay, it's okay!"

Raamatu was flustered. "Okay, okay. Go sit, I will serve it to you."

"It's fine, you don't have to worry." Gracie reassured. "I promise you it's okay."

"You are family, you no cook!"

"I won't burn the place down, it's okay." Gracie exhaustedly urged, taking the knife and cutting two pieces out and putting them onto plates. She took one plate and handed it over to Raamatu, "Here."

Raamatu made a weird face and looked at Dabir, she shook her head no, pushing the plate back. "No, no, no."

"It's good! See, look." Gracie took a bite of her piece, "No poison. It's Friday, and you work like–14 hour days. Come on, you deserve something tasty!"

Raamatu was still apprehensive, she looked at Dabir. He was quietly watching the whole interaction and could no longer stay quiet. He spoke to Raamatu in Arabic and nodded his head at her.

She cautiously picked up the plate and looked back at Gracie. She gave a shy smile and took a bite. Her eyes closed as she enjoyed the warm ooey-gooey, chocolatey goodness. "Thank you madam."

A victorious smile spread on Gracie's face, "You're welcome."

Raamatu carried her plate away to finish her dessert without being seen by Mrs. Ayad. Before she left the room, she looked at Dabir with pleading eyes, silently begging him to not report her. Dabir simply nodded his head at her.

She seemed so excited for others to try her baking, that's why he told Raamatu that it was okay. Raamatu was horribly worried she would get in trouble if she was caught eating the same food the family did.

Dabir thought that his family's treatment of the house help was absurd, so he was happy to help her feel at ease for once.

Gracie then cut another piece and turned to Dabir, "Now it's your turn, you've waited long enough."

Dabir lifted the brownie and took a bite. "It's good."

"It's good? That's it? Just good?" Gracie folded her arms, and pretended to be offended. "Do you know how much love I poured into these?!"

"I can tell, that's what makes it good." He took another bite.

"What makes it good and not great?"

"Honestly, I don't like chocolate."

"Why didn't you tell me you didn't like chocolate? I wouldn't have made you eat this super chocolatey dessert!"

"You asked me to try it, I didn't want to tell you no." Dabir answered truthfully. There wasn't a lying bone in his body.

Gracie felt her face heat up, she thought Dabir was a total sweetheart. "How was work today?"

"It was work. We are buying out a streaming platform, so...work has been work." Dabir took the last bite of his brownie. "How about you?"

"I don't work Fridays, but it was a great work week! I got a few new patients, oh!--and, I did get in contact with Hakeem, thank you for hiring him for me. I was so shocked to hear that you did that for me, that was so nice."

"It's no problem." He nodded his head and took his plate to the sink. As he passed by Gracie, she caught a whiff of his cologne. It was weirdly calming. "I'm going to the gym, I will see you around."

"You go to the gym at 10 PM? Do you even sleep?"

"I don't have any other free period than night." He walked over to pick up his suit jacket, "Good night."

Chapter 7

A few weeks had passed by since Gracie had moved into the Ayad house. She had gotten into a regular flow of living, but found herself feeling home sick. Saheed slept all day and partied all night, so it seemed. The only people Gracie really ever spoke to was Raamatu, for brief and fleeting moments, due to fear of getting in trouble. Sarai was usually away for college, but the times she was home, she and Gracie enjoyed reality tv together.

Other than those two...oddly enough, Dabir.

There were many nights where he would come home from work late when Gracie could not sleep, and in those times they would talk about the day and life at large. They even developed a new tradition of Dabir trying a new one of Gracie's recipes every Friday night. They'd eat, chat and then he would go to the gym.

To Gracie, he felt safe, he was comforting to be around. To Dabir, she felt like peace, in his hectic business life it felt good speaking to someone who was calming to the soul. A peculiar friendship but a true one nonetheless.

They had just finished up the miniature carrot cake and in-depth discussion over what his childhood was like before he came to the US. The two were saying their routine good night, because Dabir was getting ready to go to the gym.

Saheed stumbled through the front door, almost deliriously. When he regained balance, he drunkenly stormed over to where Gracie was. With fist balled up, he hollered out "WHERE HAVE YOU BEEN?!"

"Wha–" Gracie was at a loss for words, she just looked at his sloppy movement with confusion written all over her face.

"I SAW YOU! YOU WERE THERE! YOU WERE ALL OVER HIM!"

"What are you talking about!? I've been here all day." Gracie responded, feeling panicked. She didn't understand what was going on or what he was talking about. All she knew is that she could smell the alcohol on him as he advanced towards her. "What's wrong with you?!"

"OH, NOW I'M CRAZY?! I'M ALL OF THE SUDDEN SEEING THINGS?!" Saheed yelled as he quickly advanced towards Gracie. "I SAW YOU! I SAW YOU W–"

"Aht-aht-aht, stay over there! Don't walk up on me like that, Saheed!"

"SHUT UP!" Saheed yelled at the top of his lungs, scaring Gracie and waking up his parents upstairs.

He took a big step towards Gracie but was stopped by Dabir's one hand pushing him backwards. He stumbled to the ground.

Dabir began to speak to him in Arabic, he wasn't raising his voice, but his tone showed that he was chewing Saheed out. Saheed stood there, breathing hard and fast, taking in every word his brother sent his way.

Gracie was confused and concerned, and so were the parents who were now downstairs with worried looks, dressed in their matching silk pajamas. Mr. Ayad raised his arms, "What's going on?!?"

Saheed's eyes were watery and red, he turned to his parents and began speaking a mile a minute. Dabir began as well, looking straight at his father. Gracie had no clue as to what they were talking about, but after a few moments of him speaking, Mr. Ayad looked at Saheed and began to shout at him. "WHY CAN'T YOU GET IT TOGETHER?! YOU ARE A WASTE OF A MAN!"

Mrs. Ayad tearfully looked at Saheed, then scowled at her husband. She opened her arms to Saheed, "Don't yell at my son! Saheed, yalla! Yalla!"

She turned and left, hand-in-hand with Saheed. Mr. Ayad was frustrated, taking deep breaths with his hands on his hips. "Uhh, Gracie. Go sleep, okay? We will talk to him in the morning, don't worry, it's just too much alcohol, you know?"

"Yeah..." Gracie looked down, she felt so uncomfortable that she did not even want to be in her own skin.

Mr. Ayad turned his attention to Dabir. "....And Dabir, my son, adhhab 'iilaa alfirash."

When his dad left the room, it was a chilling silence between Gracie and Dabir. She was at a complete loss for words with the way Saheed just behaved. She knew that he was prone to anger when he drank too much, but at that moment, she had genuine concerns for her personal safety with him.

Her hand went over her mouth as silent tears snuck out her eyes. Dabir looked the other way, he could handle a lot, but never the sight of a woman crying.

Especially Gracie, who he had grown to really appreciate. To him, she was sweet, bright and loving, the last thing she needed was his alcoholic, lazy, younger brother.

Dabir, in a moment of being moved with great compassion, grabbed a hold of Gracie's hand and grabbed his keys from the table. He led her outside the house, to his car. He couldn't listen to her cry anymore, the gym could wait.

He opened the car door for her to get in. Gracie wiped her eyes, "Where are we going?"

"My office."

"What?"

"Trust me, please." He gently urged. After she took her seat, he closed the door. The car smelled like him. Gracie sunk deeper into her seat, already feeling calmed.

After Dabir got into the driver's side, he was off. As he drove, he noticed Gracie rub her hands together. Without a word, Dabir turned the heat up and faced the fan towards her.

The ride was about 30 minutes, and brought them into the heart of downtown in front of the skyscraper with AES's sign in front of it.

Bustling with employee's by day and club goers by night, the streets were always lively in that part of town. Dabir took a card out of his wallet and used it to scan the reader in the front of the parking garage. After the gate opened, he pulled up into a reserved spot that read:

RESERVED: Dabir A. Ayad, Managing Director of Operations

Once he had shut off the car, he had Gracie follow him to the elevator. He pressed the number for the very top floor, which was the 42nd. Once again, he was prompted to scan his work card.

It was a silent ride up. Gracie stood on the other side of the elevator as the memories of what transpired that night replayed in her mind.

The elevator door opened in front of grande French double doors, there was a golden placard with Dabir's name on it. This time, he had to punch in a pin and scan his thumbprint.

"Sheesh, y'all really take security seriously."

A green light flashed and he pushed both doors open, revealing the most spectacular office Gracie had ever seen. It was meticulously organized with a huge desk at the far wall, it put the Oval Office to shame. "You could live here."

"I already do." He grinned.

Gracie's jaw dropped, "Did you just make a joke? Oh my gosh, you cracked a joke! Was that the first time ever?" She teased, while laughing. Even in his good moods, Dabir had a tendency to be more serious and pragmatic in his speech.

"Okay, okay." He smiled widely. "Never again."

"No! At least twice a year?! Just for me?"

He looked her in the eyes for a few moments, before pulling himself back into the present moment. "I didn't bring you here to show you this, come."

He led her to a secret door that allowed them access to the unmarked 43rd floor. It was a floor with walls all made of reinforced glass, giving a panoramic view of the city.

Gracie was amazed, in wonder, her eyes traveled over all the buildings and lights against the night sky.

Dabir was also lost in thought. He sat down and stared out. He would go up there when life began to get the best of him, when it all got to be too much. He would give himself 20 minutes to think, and then go back to work. But that night was different, he wasn't thinking about work or anything else. He was just being present.

Gracie sat down on the ground, still staring outward. "I should break up with him, shouldn't I? I mean, I know that's weird to ask you, you're brothers but... This is a mistake, huh?"

He took a deep breath, but didn't respond. He knew the answer to her question, and she did too. Truthfully, he had no idea what she saw in Saheed. He would typically woo girls by flashing his wealth and charm, but Gracie wasn't motivated by money like others were.

"He's my brother."

"I know, you're right, I'm sorry. That was weird." She shook her head in embarrassment..

"It's not." He sat down on the floor next to her. "It's not weird. But... It doesn't matter what I think, Gracie...At the end of the day, he's still my brother."

"Yeah." Gracie took a deep breath. She thought about how horribly Saheed would talk about Dabir. Yet even in a justifiable moment, Dabir refused to speak against Saheed. "I won't be in a rush to make a decision now, I guess... I'll—I'll think about it."

The pair sat quietly, comfortably. Thinking, being and watching the city from forty-three floors in the sky.

Chapter 8

Some days went by, and things were back to normal. Well, as normal as it could get.

Saheed's drunken night came and went, there was no discussion of what had transpired.

No conversation, nothing.

Gracie had a particularly rough day at work. There was a patient in the lactation center that went into a depressive episode due to her perceived weak bond with her baby. Gracie was called in to de-escalate. Moments like that always triggered an adrenaline response in Gracie, it took rest and time to recoup.

She had time to take a quick shower and change into something comfy after work, but had to hurry so that she could eat dinner with the family. Dabir often did not eat dinner with the family, due to being at work. Saheed would usually speed through his meal and be out the door to the clubs. That night, Gracie didn't care what he did, she just wanted to rest. Gracie had every intent of getting through the dinner as quickly as possible, calling her mom and going to sleep.

She was wearing a sweat suit, her glasses and a high ponytail in a much more 'lax look than she usually had. Mrs. Ayad stood in the kitchen micromanaging the kitchen staff, she looked Gracie up and down and looked away, Gracie didn't care. She was far too exhausted to mind the judgmental look.

Mr. Ayad, on the other hand, was always happy to see Gracie. "My daughter, how was your work today?"

"It was a crazy day, if I'm being honest." She breathed out, taking her seat at the dining table.

"Oh! A crazy person?"

"No, not that, no one there is clinically able to be called crazy so to speak, it was a challenging moment with a challenging patient, that's all."

"What happened?"

She smiled at him and shook her head, "Patient confidentiality, sorry."

Sarai listened in, with a star-struck look on her face. "That's so cool that you are a therapist. There really does need to be more POC in mental health."

"POC?" Mr. Ayad was unfamiliar with the terminology.

"People of color, Baba."

"Oh! So...black?" His eyes darted to Gracie, "Is that the correct way to say it?"

Mrs. Ayad cut in as she took her seat next to her husband, "Yes, habibi. It's black."

There was a venom in the words as Mrs. Ayad spoke. Sarai rolled her eyes and gave Gracie an apologetic look.

Shortly after, Saheed joined them at the table, and Raamatu with the rest of the kitchen help brought out the elaborate feast. Gracie was not going to complain about it, she was grateful after all, but the surplus of food cooked every night...was getting old. The family was not even able to finish half the amount that was cooked, tons were thrown away every night. To make it worse, Mrs. Ayad did not believe it was right for staff to eat the same meals that the family did, so they would have to cook the ridiculous requested amount, serve it, throw it away, clean up all the dishes and then get to go look for dinner for themselves.

To everyone's surprise, halfway through the silent dinner, Dabir joined them. Mr. Ayad looked as if he could have fainted from the excitement. He stood up from his seat at the head of the table, and offered it to Dabir. "Son, please, sit."

"It's okay, Baba." He calmly responded, taking a seat next to Sarai, across from Gracie. They caught a glimpse of each other and Gracie gave him a reassuring smile. A small smile spread on his face as well, before he took off his suit jacket to comfortably begin eating.

Saheed caught sight of the little interaction Dabir and Gracie shared. He felt instantly on edge, and felt the need to claim what he felt was his.

He reached into his pocket and pulled out a tiny blue box . He didn't buy it for Gracie originally, but she didn't need to know that. Afterall, he could always buy another pair. He put it on the table and slid it towards Gracie, "Check it out baby."

"What's this?" She asked, taking the box in her hands. As she opened it up, 2 carat sapphire earrings looked back at her. They were set on 18k white gold, and the back of the post had a white diamond. She never saw anything like that in her life. "Oh my goodness...This is–"

"I told you I'd always take care of you!" He boasted, he turned to Dabir. "What do you think? How do they look, 'big bro'? Guess how much they cost me? $40,000! AND I paid in cash."

Gracie let out a breath and set the box back on the table, his gloating and over the top flashing of wealth made her uncomfortable.

Dabir simply took another bite of his food, he wasn't about to play into Saheed's theatrics, Dabir fully understood that Saheed is not reasonable and therefore can not be reasoned with. He took his jacket off the back of his chair, got up and left. Saheed felt victorious as his brother walked away, Gracie felt distraught.

Mr. Ayad also watched Dabir leave, the sight made Mr. Ayad's heart heavy. That was one of the first times in years Dabir had sat with the family and it pained him that it was over so soon. Mr. Ayad wondered what was different that he would now be willing, his eyes landing on Gracie.

The dinner carried on in a cryptic silence.

After dinner, Gracie sat outside enjoying the cool summer breeze, and talking to her mom over the phone. She planned to go visit her mom over the weekend, she missed her greatly.

Saheed eventually joined her outside, he draped his arm over her shoulder. A huge change from his recent behavior, his tone was sweet and peaceable. "Are you okay?"

"I'm okay, I miss my mom." She answered truthfully. "I'm thinking of going there this weekend. I miss my friends too."

"I wanted to talk to you about that actually..."

"What happened?" She looked him in the eyes, he had her full attention.

"I don't like you being friends with that Alexis girl. You shouldn't be friends with girls like that." He avoided eye contact as he spoke, Gracie noticed.

"You only met her once. I'm not sure how you know anything about her."

"How do you mean?"

"You said I shouldn't be friends with girls like her... What is a girl like her?"

"Oh come on, you know." He fumbled over his words and made random hand gestures. "Look. I just don't like the girl, I don't trust her. I don't want anyone causing you headaches."

"You cause me headaches."

"Yeah, everything is my fault, like usual. Would you just listen to me?! I'm only warning you because I care."

"Okay, message received. I will keep my distance." Gracie sighed eye, rolling her eyes for the cherry on top. "If that's all, I'm going to bed."

"Did you finally quit your job like I told you to?"

"Do you even care about me? Like...At all? You sleep all day, drink all night, the few times we even speak to each other we are bickering. What are we doing?"

"Of course we are bickering! You are always cuddled up under MY BROTHER!"

"Cuddled up. Wow." Gracie folded her arms. "He's kind and considerate. We aren't cuddling up, and you know that."

"You expect me to believe that? No, like really?"

"I want to be with someone who wants to be with me. Someone loving and gentle and sweet. Which is how you were when we were dating long distance, Saheed you've changed. I don't know how much longer I can do this with you treating me this way. I'm sorry if you feel uncomfortable with your brother and I's friendship, I really am, BUT maybe you should spend more time with me if you dislike it so much."

"Go to bed before I lose it!"

Gracie huffed, her blood was hot. He still wasn't hearing her. He still did not see how close she was to being done. "Good night."

Chapter 9

The following day was a better one. Gracie was dressed to the nines and ready to help change some lives.

She cleared out her schedule so she could manage back to back group therapy sessions. It was fast-paced, yet conversational. The work day went by quickly.

As Gracie walked out her work place, she saw a little old lady pushing her churro cart along. Gracie gasped in pleasant surprise. The first thing that came to mind was Dabir, she just knew he would love one.

She bubbled over in excitement and walked over as quickly as her heels would allow. "Hi! Do you have any more?"

"Yes, how many do you want?"

"Fourteen, please! Can you put it into a box or something?" She reached into the purse on her arm and pulled out cash. She wanted to have one with Dabir, but also enough for everyone in the family and the staff

After the transaction, she practically skipped into the car where Hakeem waited for her. "Back home?"

"No, can you actually take me to AES?"

Hakime gave a confused expression but shrugged. "As you wish."

They were then stuck in traffic for 45 minutes, it was rush hour. It felt like all of eternity before they finally pulled up in front of the headquarters for the major media conglomerate.

Gracie stepped out of the car, and dialed Dabir's number as she walked towards the lobby entrance. It seemed as if she had just walked into wall-street, with all the hustle and bustle.

"Gracie, what's wrong?" Dabir asked. His heart skipped a beat from worry, people usually only would call him when there was a problem.

Gracie couldn't contain the smile on her face. "Nothing's wrong! Are you busy right now?"

"Is everything okay?"

"Everything is fine, Dabir, I'm not trying to worry you." Her big brown eyes continued to take in the room. "Come to the lobby, I have something for you."

"You're downstairs?"

"Mhm! I figured it was best to call, I knew I wasn't going to get past the elevator without all that security stuff you guys have."

"Oh. Okay. Security will let you through in a moment. You can go to the front desk."

She wore a soft pink dress and matching heels, her hair was straight and down her back. She felt like a black barbie as she walked through the sea of professionals all dressed in gray or black. It didn't help that she was holding a box filled with an obscene amount of churros.

A few moments passed before a gentleman dressed in black approached Gracie and led her to the elevators. He had to punch in lengthy passcodes to get them in, up and out again. When they got outside the office, he knocked loudly on the solid wood door.

Dabir opened the door, with his eyes on Gracie immediately. He pulled his gaze away from her to look up at the security official. "That will be all, thank you."

The man nodded and turned to leave. Gracie was let into the office, it was just as remarkable as it was last time they were there. "What can I do for you?" His tone was warm and kind, he pulled a chair back for her to sit in.

"Oh nothing....Except! Rate these on a scale from one two ten!" Gracie opened the box displaying the golden-brown, cinnamony-sugar delights. Dabir reached in to grab one, but Gracie slammed the box shut. "Aren't you going to ask what it is first?"

He smirked. "Okay. What is this?"

She couldn't fight back her smile either, "It's a Latin American dessert, 'cause we are going international now! It's called churro, and from what I know, it's a fried dough with cinnamon and sugar. Inside is soft, the outside is crunchy, it's great and you will love it."

"You came all this way for me to eat doughnut?"

"It's NOT a doughnut, but yes, I came all this way for you to get fat with me." She answered victoriously.

"Can I eat it now?"

"Go for it, D."

He took a big bite, and followed it up with another. He gave Gracie a silent thumbs up. "Yes."

She quickly covered her mouth to avoid showing chewed up churro. Something about his yes, cracked her up. "Exactly! It is a yes! I knew I was going to find a non-Arab dessert you like!"

"It reminds me of Sahlab. I used to have it all the time before I moved to America."

"What's in it?"

"It's—how do I describe it, like a milk pudding."

"Milk pudding? How does that remind you of a churro?"

"It reminds me, I didn't say they were similar."

Well... Maybe it tastes better than it sounds, do they sell any nearby?"

"I'll make it for you."

Her eyebrow raised, "Since when do you cook? Or eat for that matter! Have you even eaten anything besides this? It's almost 7 and I know you've probably been here since like 6 in the morning."

"There's a lot to do here."

"There's something every day, but you still have to take care of yourself. Come on, let's go grab dinner with the rest."

"I don't like family dinners. You don't either, I'm not going."

"I never said I don't like family dinners!" She defended before immediately lowering her shoulders, "Is it that obvious?"

Dabir snickered. "There is a place down the street I like, let's go there."

"Deal deal deal." She followed him out then abruptly stopped, "Wait! I forgot! I have to take these churros back to the house because Raamatu is going to love them. That woman's got a big time sweet tooth on her!"

He smiled from ear to ear, his green eyes twinkling. "As you wish."

Chapter 10

Time progressed on, and soon enough it was the weekend. Gracie had gone to see her mother and friends. I felt like she had not seen Saheed in days. Why bother staying at home when he was never there? They spent no time together and didn't even speak. The relationship felt like poison to Gracie.

Back at the Ayad house, the house was more dull without Gracie's bright and bubbly personality. Her smile alone lit up rooms and hearts.

Mr. Ayad had summoned Dabir into his study, right as Dabir was preparing to go to his own home office to get some work done. Dabir knew that his father and Saheed had been down there talking all morning.

Dabir got into the room and saw Saheed kneeling on the ground weeping, as his dad paced in a worried and angry fashion. In Arabic, Dabir asked "What is all this?"

"My son, please, sit. We need your help. Your idiot brother–" Mr. Ayad raised his hand to strike Saheed, causing him to flinch. "Your brother has brought shame to this house."

Dabir took in a deep breath and let it out, whenever Saheed acted out, everyone would turn to Dabir to make it better. He was always Mr. Fix-It, but this issue was about way more than he could handle.

"Saheed! Tell him what you did!"

"Why do I have to-"

"Shut up! He's your only hope!" Mr. Ayad shouted, before plopping down into his chair. He felt faint.

Saheed knew this was true. Afterall, a big part of what Dabir did for a living was negotiating multi-million dollar contracts, he could reason with anyone. He might have hated Dabir, but he needed him now more than ever.

"SPEAK!" Mr. Ayad screamed.

"Baba." Dabir called, firmly but calmly. He didn't want to get caught in the middle of a yelling match between his father and Saheed.

"Okay, okay. I won't yell." Mr. Ayad assured, his eyes cut back to Saheed. "Speak. Now."

"Fine." Saheed wiped his face and sat back on the chair, his head turned in the opposite direction from where Dabir. He cleared his throat. "I...I got someone pregnant."

Re-hearing the admission, Mr. Ayad felt sick to his stomach all over again. Dabir felt a pang in his chest. Both Mr. Ayad and Dabir were absolutely gutted for Gracie, they were abhorred.

Dabir didn't understand how Saheed could be so repeatedly and consistently stupid. He felt as if he was about to lose his mind, he stood up abruptly. "This is not my concern, Baba. Let him figure it out."

"No! Please! Please, my son. Your brother needs you, without your help she will surely leave. Gracie would make the perfect wife! Beautiful, smart, kind, everything! She must be kept happy." Mr. Ayad urged.

"What is the expectation? He needs to deal with his own decision."

"My son, wait! You and Gracie seem to be very close, no? Talk to her for your brother."

Saheed looked over for the first time, the brothers eyes were locked. Even in such a desperate moment, he felt anger and jealousy at the thought of Gracie being near Dabir.

With eyes still on Saheed, Dabir said "He needs to be a man."

"I AM A MAN!"

"A man wouldn't do this." Dabir's face was hot, he took a deep breath to calm down before he continued speaking. "This is foolish and childish... What do you expect me to do? Beg Gracie for you?"

"Gracie doesn't have to know anything... well she shouldn't have to know. We still have time! The girl is trying to out me, but I'm thinking we can get it under control for the right amount of dollar signs..? You know?"

"So now that you've blown all your money, you want me to pay your mistress off for you. Is that what you are asking me?"

"I just need you to get it under control for me, bro."

"What does control look like to you?"

"You know..." Saheed scoffed, "Don't act like you've never paid a girl off to get an abortion."

"La qaddar allah." (Translation: God forbid)

"We just have to pay her I! It's just that she's-- she's just asking for too much, you know?! She's being so greedy, you know?!"

"I don't." Dabir sighed. "I don't, Saheed. I don't understand why you did this."

Saheed shot up from where he was seated, frustrated. He felt like Dabir was looking down on him. "Why do you always look at me like that?! You think you're better than me!"

Mr. Ayad snapped, "Hey! Don't talk to my son like that! You MUST respect him!"

"Baba." Dabir called in a warning tone.

Saheed scowled. "Whatever man! It's always my son this, my son that, I'm your son too! Why don't you treat me like that!?"

"Like what?! You spend all my money on women and drinks, and you think it is Dabir who has special treatment?! Have I ever scolded you? Have I lifted my hand against you?! You have had all that you've wanted since the womb! And what have I asked of you, Saheed, the only thing I've asked?! All I asked was that you get married! Find a good woman! Have a family! I gave you my word that if you did that, I would never make you work a day in your life! But look now, look how you've disgraced the Ayad name! The one reasonable girl and you have destroyed the hope for your future with her!"

"I DON'T want to be married! You caused this! How come you never forced Dabir to find someone?!"

"Because Dabir—! Dabir is...I've never had to worry about Dabir." Mr. Ayad paused, the room falling silent. He tearfully looked at Dabir. "Dabir is different, he's always been able to look after himself."

Saheed sneered, "Yeah that's right. Precious Dabir...Your special little orphan boy."

"Saheed!"

"You favor him because you feel bad for him! It's not my fault his mom died and you married mine! I wish that when she died she took him with her!"

The room got fiery hot. Mr. Ayad couldn't even be angry at Saheed, he was too busy fearing for Saheed's life. Dabir never showed violent inclinations, but this was a moment Mr. Ayad feared that Dabir would beat the brakes off Saheed.

On Dabir's maternal side of the family, the men were on average 6'5 and built solid. That trait did not skip Dabir. He towered over his family, especially Saheed. As a child Dabir learned early on that he could not get involved in the childish rough housing that other kids enjoyed, for fear of causing real harm.

He walked over to Saheed who was filled with regret but too stubborn to do anything about it. Dabir put one of his hands on Saheed's shoulder, "I will let it go this time, and this time only. Let this be the last mention of my mother from your mouth."

-

Miles and miles away, Gracie was laughing it up with her mom and friends over a homemade Nigerian food. It was completely unbeknownst to her all of the drama and mayhem going on at the Ayad household. She snapped a picture of her food some time ago and sent it to Dabir. She checked her phone and was disappointed that there was still no response.

"You just can't get enough of him, can you?"

"Huh? What do you mean?!"

"We see you checking your phone! Saheed will text you when he gets a chance girl, dang!" Leni teased.

"Oh, ha, yeah." Gracie put her phone down, face now flushed. "So what's been new with y'all? It feels like it has been five-ever."

Becca swished around her wine and raised a mischievous eyebrow. "Did you hear about Alexis?"

"No? Is she okay?" Gracie worriedly asked.

"Is she okay...Yeah, she's okay! The girl is pregnant! And rumor is baby daddy is stacking, look." Becca opened up her social media feed and went to the top pic. It showed Alexis smiling ear to ear holding an early pregnancy ultrasound.

"Aw, she looks so ha—..." Gracie paused. Her eyes landed on the earrings that Alexis wore in the picture. Gracie's eyes squinted at the sight.

2+2 was immediately equaling 4.

They were the exact same ones that Saheed had gifted her. At the bottom of the post announcing her pregnancy, Alexis said

"Also, I want to give a MAJOR S/O to @lekkilandjewlers for helping me and bae with these beautiful custom earrings!"

Gracie went straight to @lekkilandjewelers page. She didn't even need to scroll before she saw all that she needed. At the top of the page was a picture the jeweler took with Saheed. The caption read:

"There's money and then there's money money! Had to hook up my boy @sayad with some of the finest Sapphires money can buy! It was so nice he had to buy it twice!"

"You okay?" Becca asked after seeing Gracie's face fall.

"One second y'all." Gracie put the phone down.

She then got up from the dining table and took off into her mom's bedroom. Her mom was watching tv in bed, the second she saw Gracie's face she sat straight up. "What happened? Omo mi, what is it?!"

"Mummy, he got someone pregnant. That fool cheated on me with Alexis!"

Chapter 11

About a week had gone by since the drama unfurled, and Gracie was over it.

It's not that she didn't feel betrayed or hurt, she felt both and very deeply. It was more so that she was simply over it. She was over the disrespect, the anger, and fake friendship... Though it hurt, she felt lighter with the dead weight removed.

She had spent the week with her mom debriefing from the shock. Gracie had put her phone on DND, and was not speaking to anyone other than her mother, her patients and Jesus.

Gracie had just wrapped up her last patient for the day and was completing the visit note. That patient was moved on to Gracie's schedule last minute so she was having to work a bit later than usual. Lately she did not mind working later, it kept her mind busy and out of her feelings.

A few quiet knocks sounded from her office door.

"I know Rhonda, I'm wrapping up." She let out a defeated breath, and pushed a loose curl behind her ear. Rhonda never liked leaving until everyone else was out the building, usually she would give Gracie a pass, but lately she had been on Gracie's case about leaving timely. "I don't mind locking up, you can go."

The door creaked open, Gracie shook her head in annoyance and continued to type, not once looking up. "I don't know what to tell you, it's going to be another 5 or 10."

"Are you expecting somebody?" A deep, sultry, yet familiar soul-warming voice asked.

Gracie's fiercely-fast, typing fingers froze. She could recognize that comforting voice from anywhere. Her eyes slowly moved upwards from her computer, to the dashing green eyes of Dabir. She did not know why he was there, but deep down she was happy to see someone who grew to be a good friend. Her heart fluttered at the sight of his face.

But at the same time...

It was awkward. Afterall, she had just gotten out of a relationship with his brother, after experiencing a horrendous betrayal. The thought popped into Gracie's head: Is he only here to convince me to go back? Do they have him here doing Saheed's dirty work?

Her guard instantly went up.

"What are you doing here?"

Dabir was shocked by her harsh tone, but he was understanding. He figured she would not be happy to see anyone from the Ayad family ever again, yet he could not bring himself to let life move on as if she had never happened in his life.

"Well?" Gracie asked, scooting back from her desk to cross her arms and her legs. She felt herself on defense mode, as she waited to hear him make excuses for his brother.

Moments passed in silence, finally, Dabir broke it, "Have you been okay?"

"Have I been okay? No. YOUR brother got my friend pregnant, so no, I haven't been okay. Did you really come all this way to ask that?"

"I did."

Her frown fell, "You came just to see if I am okay?"

"You weren't answering my calls. I came to see that you were okay."

"Oh." Gracie's arms dropped down to her side, her legs uncrossed. Even her shoulders fell in surrender. She knew that she couldn't be upset with Dabir, he wasn't her enemy. Her pride was still hurt from being humiliated publicly. How could she have let herself get played so badly? "Okay, well, I haven't felt like talking, so...As you see, I'm fine, you can go."

"I'm relieved to see that you are okay, take care of yourself." With that he turned and left.

Dabir left for Gracie's sake, not his own. What he really wanted to do was pull Gracie into his arms and not let go until he was sure she was actually okay. He wanted to take her to dinner somewhere small and quiet. He wanted to apologize to her for ever getting her heart caught up with an idiot like Saheed in the first place. But he knew he couldn't do that. More than anything, he wanted her to be happy, even if it meant he had to leave.

He left the building the same way he came in, with a wide-eyed Rhonda oogling at him. He wore a perfectly tailored navy suit with a white shirt, his gold watch shined in the light.

"I've seen you before, you're her fiancé's brother right?" Rhonda asked as she gave her best flirtatious smirk she could muster.

Dabir looked back, he did not even notice her there, his mind was still wrapped around his conversation with Gracie. He was unsure as to why Rhonda was questioning him.

"My oh my, your daddy sure does know how to make 'em!" She stood up and put a hand on her shapely hip. "You got a girl?"

"Have a good night." Dabir replied politely but firmly, continuing on his way.

Meanwhile, Gracie was rushing to get her heels on and get out the door. She did not want the potentially last interaction between her and Dabir to be soured, she felt horrible for kicking him out the way she did.

She hustled as fast as she could. Rhonda was up front with a big pout on her face. "Did he already leave?!"

Rhonda was in her feeling over being turned down by Dabir, she was praying to her lucky stars that he would be her ticket out of the workforce. "He's gone, just like my chances."

Gracie's eyebrow raised, "What are you talking about? Actually hold that thought, I need to find him before he leaves."

Outside, the parking lot was empty, Dabir's car was nowhere to be found. Gracie sighed, and pulled out her phone.

It rang, and it rang, but to Gracie's delight there was an answer. "Hey, come back, I want you to go home with me."

Chapter 12

W ith one hand holding her phone, the other slammed against her forehead. She cringed in her own skin. Adrenaline filled, she had told Dabir that she wanted him to come home with her, when she was really trying to tell him to drive her home so they could talk.

Dabir was silent on the other end, his face heated up. He was on his way home, but pulled over as soon as he saw the call come through.

"I meant I want you to drive me home. It didn't come out right, I just wanted the--sorry, I'll stop talking. Please take a ride with me if you aren't busy."

"Wait inside, I'm just down the street."

A small smile spread on Gracie's face as she disconnected the call. She sat down on the edge of the fountain to wait for him. Her phone was now off of do not disturb for the first time in a week.

Unfortunately, that meant that the floodgates were now opened.

From Saheed alone, she had 66 text messages. The messages went from nonchalant, to panicked, from panicked to nonchalant again. It was a joke.

She scrolled through a few messages from the day that Alexis announced her pregnancy

"Babe, let's take a trip.me and you, no phones, no tv. How does Paris sound? We can fly out 2night."

"Babe??"

"Hey, where are you?!"

"Bonjour sexy!"

"Don't believe anything you hear!!! It's ALL lies!"

"ANSWER YOUR ******* PHONE!"

"Let's get married this week, I don't want to wait a year <3 why wait?"

Gracie stopped reading, Saheed was a mess and she was shocked that she did not notice it earlier. She shook her head as she put her phone back in her purse. She still had to go and pack up her belongings, but needed to muster the strength to go back.

It didn't take long before Dabir pulled up, he parked the car and rounded it so he could open the door for Gracie, as per usual. "You were supposed to wait inside."

"I like the evening breeze." Gracie retorted, she stood in front of Dabir who was waiting for her to get in the car so that he could close the door. "Thank you for coming back, I know you must be tired to be doing this after work."

"It's okay, I left work early."

"D, it doesn't count if you still worked over eight hours." Gracie sat down and took a deep breath in, she loved the smell of Dabir's car, it smelled just like him. The smell made her feel safe.

When Dabir got in, he took Gracie's address and input it to the GPS. They began to talk about their respective work days and all that had happened in the past week, both of them ignored discussing the obvious elephant in the room.

Finally, Around the halfway point of the drive, with a mischievous smirk on her face, Gracie poked fun at the anything but laughable situation. "So it looks like your dad and mom are finally getting that grand baby they wanted, huh?"

Dabir shook his head, he was much less amused than Gracie was.

"Come on, if I'm laughing about it, you don't get to be serious."

"It's not funny to me, Gracie, the child will suffer."

"Cause of Saheed or Alexis?" Gracie snickered, those two were a joke to her."

"I can't speak about the girl, I don't know her. All I can speak on is what I know."

"Oh yeah right, Dabir, I know your parents probably have that girl moving in as we speak. They are probably overjoyed."

"Gracie."

"Yeah, yeah, I know. I'll stop."

Dabir shook his head, he looked between her and the road, "I'm sorry this happened to you."

"Thank you, D...It's I guess kind of embarrassing, you know? I spent so much time invested in the relationship, it was a huge let down to finally come face to face with the truth. I spent 8 months in a long distance relationship with someone that I guess I never knew. I learned the truth the hard way." She shrugged, "That he just wasn't that into me after all."

"It sounds very painful."

"That gut-wrenching pain part is over actually, now I'm left with the disgust and regret for even wasting my time in the first place. Literally it's giving me the ick. I don't know what it was about him, something about him pulled me in, I guess. All that glitters isn't gold, huh?" She shifted in her seat. "And you can let me know if it gets weird talking about your brother, I get it. It's a little weird talking to you about it for me too. Who wants to listen to their brother's ex rant about the break up?"

"You are my friend before you are anyone's ex, I would tell you if I was not comfortable."

"Is this you giving me the green light to go there?"

"Yes."

And oh...Gracie went there.

For the duration of the ride, she spent it going on and off about the failed relationship. This was her first time really opening up about how she felt in detail and every word came out her mouth like daggers. It was as if she was finally able to take off her therapist hat, and be a patient for once.

As he pulled into the driveway of the home Gracie shared with her mom, Dabir looked Gracie in the eyes as she finished her rant. He felt in no rush to go anywhere.

The heaviness of the conversation was beginning to catch up with Gracie. She looked down towards her lap and used her wrist to wipe away the silent tears. Dabir's heart broke at the sight.

"Gosh, I'm sorry, D.... I didn't mean to get so emotional, I wouldn't have talked about it if I knew I was going to cry like this in front of you, it's embarrassing.."

"You're okay, Gracie, you're fine."

"And I'm sorry for making you drive me home, I just felt like–"

"Hey, it's okay."

"I mean you say that but I feel really bad, I'm sorry for dragging you into my mess. Who wants to sit and listen to a girl go on and on about--"

"When will you stop apologizing? You've never forced me to be or do anything. I'm around you because I want to be around you."

Gracie wiped her tears away, a shy smile visible on her face, she couldn't help it. Gracie tried to change the subject. "Are you hungry?"

"What do you want to eat?"

"Hmm, I think it's time you try Nigerian food, come in."

Chapter 13

That weekend, Gracie woke up feeling like she had a new lease on life. She started the day with her prayers, devotion and beauty routine. With her hair as smooth and straighter than ever, she put on her favorite yellow sundress. Her makeup was applied flawlessly, with shiny pink lips and beautiful hybrid lashes.

When Gracie walked downstairs, her mom's jaw dropped at the sight of her. "Ah ah, where are you going looking like this, Iya?"

Gracie twirled, "I look good, huh?"

"Good? You are looking great! Just like me when I was in my twenties! Where are you going?"

"I'm finally going to go pack out my stuff, and then I need to give back this ring and these stupid earrings he gave."

"Haa, are you sure? If you sell it, ha, for even 3 years you won't need to work."

"I'm sure mummy, you don't know how petty he can get. It's best that the chapter is closed for good, and that no traces are left behind."

"That useless boy." Gracie's mom scowled. "Ode. I regret that it was him and not his older one."

"Mummy!" Gracie's face heated up, "Now why would you say that?"

"What? It's true! I'm not allowed to talk again? See how sweet and gentle he was the other night when he came over! As rich as he is, he washed his own plate after eating. If it was that idiot, chaiiii, the whole neighborhood would hear him talking yappa, yappa, yappa."

"He was pretty chatty, huh?" Gracie snickered. "What a nightmare. That's why it's with joy I drop off this ring."

"How are you getting there? Have you called a taxi?"

"Yup! They should be outside, I'll be home in a few hours." Gracie hugged her mom and went about her day.

Not too long after, Gracie was pulling up to the long driveway of the Ayad family. The sight alone gave her a stomach ache, she knew that she very well may be walking into a hostile environment. Gracie felt much less prepared to see the family now that she was actually there.

With a big, deep breath in and out, Gracie made her way to the front door.

The sudden cold feet she had was unbearable. In a last minute effort to avoid attention, she sent Dabir a text asking him to open the door for her. She felt as though ringing the doorbell would elicit unwanted attention, and she knew if she saw him she would feel much more grounded.

After sending the message, several agonizing minutes went by before the sound of the deadbolt unlocking pulled Gracie back into reality.

Dabir opened the door. It was Gracie's first time seeing him not in business attire. Fresh out the shower, his wavy hair was wet and his clothes casual. For the first time, Gracie was able to notice the width of his biceps, her eyes traveled to the veins on his large hands. Has he always looked like this? She wondered to herself.

While Gracie absent-mindedly was checking out Dabir, he was using everything in his power to avoid doing the same. Gracie had always looked beautiful to him, to everyone for that matter. She exuded feminine energy everywhere she went, and of all the things one could call her, it could never be ugly.

But there was something different about that day.

Maybe it was the way the sweet and subtle scent of her perfume flooded his senses, or the way her yellow dress contrasted against her deep, brown skin. Perhaps it was how soft her skin looked. Who could tell? It very well may have been her big brown doll-eyes looking up at him. He looked the other way and asked, "Today's the day, huh?"

"I guess so!.. Gotta' get all my things, so you guys can turn my room into a nursery." She joked.

Dabir let out a quick breath, it still was not a laughing matter to him, he probably would never find it funny. He opened the door wider so that Gracie could pass through. "Just so you know, they are all home."

"I'll be in and out, hopefully gone before anyone even notices that I'm h–"

"Gracie!" Mr. Ayad yelled in excitement and shock. He was rounding the corner from his study and heard her voice. His heart skipped a beat when he saw her in the flesh. "Come here, come! Tonight we will feast in order to welcome you home! A proper celebration!"

Mr. Ayad wanted nothing more than for a girl like Gracie to end up with his sons. She was beautiful, kind, educated and it didn't hurt that she was of faith and held on to her convictions. He made his way across the room to give her a hug, but stopped in his tracks when he noticed Gracie's expression.

"Mr. Ayad, I–"

"Gracie, no! No, no no, don't tell me bad news this morning."

"I'm sorry, I just can't do it. I can't be with him anymore."

"Why? Why?! Saheed is VERY sorry, he will never disappoint you again! I will make sure of it. Please.Try to forgive him. In your Christian Bible it says to forgive, no?"

"Sir, this isn't a forgiveness matter. I'm able to forgive him, but that doesn't mean I have to ever speak to him again. God doesn't want me to be subjected to all that." She put her hands up, "He got a close friend of mine pregnant, that's kind of a big deal, I'm sorry."

Mr. Ayad looked at Dabir with pleading eyes, silently begging for him to help convince her. Dabir shook his head no, there was no convincing. Mr. Ayad was defeated and now desperate for his son's sake. "Gracie, you name the amount, anything. It can be a house, a car, whatever you want. Anything."

"This is really uncomfortable for me."

Dabir tensed up, he was not about to sit back and watch his dad pester Gracie about Saheed anymore, Dabir felt offended that his father would even attempt to pay her off. He shot his dad a warning look, and in that moment Mr. Ayad threw in the towel. He took a step out of Gracie's way and allowed her to continue with her plans to go and pack.

When she left the room, Mr. Ayad looked at Dabir, "Why is she being stubborn about this?"

"Baba, is that the question you would ask if it were Sarai in her shoes?"

"It's different, Dabir, don't ask questions like that." He sighed, leaning his weight against the kitchen counter, he then looked Dabir up and down noticing the casual dressing. "You're not going into work today?"

"It's Saturday."

"Of course. But... Usually you go everyday? I hope there's no problem."

"No problem, Baba."

For a brief and fleeting moment, Dabir was re-offended. How could his dad be shocked that he's not working his usual seven day work week, when his other son has never worked a day in his life? Dabir shook off the offense, he never wanted to hold on to the negative feelings as they only slowed him down.

Chapter 14

It was about two hours of undistracted work before Gracie had packed all of her belongings up. Though it did feel bittersweet, she had already grown an attachment to the help staff, Sarai, Mr. Ayad, Dabir... Even though the long commute to work had become something she started to enjoy, she looked forward to chit-chatting with Mr. Hakime about therapy modalities; he found them all so fascinating.

Opening the bedroom door wide, Gracie held her head high and began pulling her luggage along. In the hallway Raamatu saw her, she looked both ways and sneakily approached Gracie, doing her best to avoid being seen by Mrs. Ayad.

Gracie opened her arms wide and the two embraced. Raamatu deeply valued and appreciated Gracie's kindness.. She was the first person other than Dabir to treat her like a human in that house. Raamatu's eyes watered as she reminisced on all of the times Gracie had come to her defense or snuck her a dessert. "You deserve better."

"YOU deserve better, so much better." Gracie noticed the tears on Raamatu's face, and wiped them away. "Oh please don't do that! I'm not dying, Raamatu, please don't cry."

"All of us on staff had prayed things would work out, if you were here to stay, things would be so much better."

Gracie felt a rush of sadness and guilt hit her. She saw the way that Mrs. Ayad and Saheed treated the staff, it was disgusting, but still Gracie knew she had to put herself first in this situation. "I'm sorry, but you know I can't stay with him."

"By God's grace, you will get an even better man for a husband. When that time comes, let me know, I will come work for you."

Gracie hugged Raamatu tightly and gave her a kiss on the cheek. Saying goodbye was always tough, but this one really hurt her.

Gracie carried on with her luggage, Raamatu helping her with a bag as well. All she had to do was pass through the living room and kitchen, and she would be free of the Ayad family.

Right as she was just about to open the front door, from the top of the staircase Saheed saw her.

He ran down as fast as he could "Gracie!"

When Gracie saw him coming, she took her bag from Raamatu and said, "Take care of yourself."

She quickly took her things and went out the front door, the last thing she wanted to deal with is Saheed's sob story, just him saying her name made her sick.

Outside, Gracie's taxi was late. She knew it would be just moments before Saheed caught up,

"Great." She muttered under her breath.

"Gracie! Baby, wait!" Saheed called out just a few feet behind her.

Gracie's eyes rolled, as she turned back to face him. "What could you possibly want from me? Haven't you taken enough time from me?!"

"Baby, you haven't picked up any of my calls?! Why?!"

"Why? Is that a real question?"

He sealed his lips shut and nodded his head, "That was a dumb question, sorry, just—just, please, come back inside, let's talk this through."

"Everything I need is out here." She coldly responded, "Your ring is on my nightstand, It should fit Alexis just fine though."

"Baby,forget about her! What happened, means nothing—I was stupid, okay? It's just that I–I I'm a man! I have needs, Gracie, you insist on waiting until marriage and it's just not easy for me, no guy could do that!"

"Oh my gosh." Gracie put a hand over her mouth, pretending to be sad, "You're so right! I'm so sorry, Saheed! I shouldn't have been so clear and upfront about my personal values. This is all my fault! I'm so sorry I made you get my FRIEND PREGNANT, you dog."

"So what, you're going to throw away all that we have over this?" He paused, growing in frustration. He took a step back and pointed to the mansion and cars that surrounded him. "You're going to give up all this? This is the life you're quitting because of one mistake that we can fix?!"

"Yup."

Saheed grabbed her arm. "Just like that?! You're going to let another girl come in?! Gonna give up this dream life?! All the shoes, bags, diamonds, vacations, wi–"

"That's the difference between me and you. I don't worship money, I worship God." She snatched her arm away from him. "I'm happily forfeiting this so-called dream life to Alexis. Let's see how well she does with your six personalities."

The look of desperation turned into Saheed's familiar look of unjustified anger. "This is your last chance."

"And I'm telling you I don't want it! Leave me alone, go read a parenting book or something."

"I don't even want to be with her!!!" He shouted harshly, causing Gracie to flinch.

In the nick of time the taxi cab rolled up. Gracie was more than grateful to be ending the conversation at that point. She walked her bags over as the driver helped her put her luggage in the back. Saheed watched silently.

And just like that, she was gone. With no more room in her heart for Saheed ever again.

Inside the house, it was quiet, as if everyone had gone into grieving. They were all in the living room, with the tv playing some movie in the background. Mr. Ayad sat like someone who had witnessed death, while his wife who was next to him, smirked victoriously, sipping on her tea.

Sarai typed away on her phone in annoyance, ranting to her friends about how annoying her family was.

And then there was Dabir.

He did not feel sad to see Gracie go, because frankly, this was for the best. Saheed would have only weighed her down in life. Dabir would miss coming home from work to see her at the house, but by no means would he prefer that she continue to suffer in a horrible relationship for his selfish sake.

No longer wanting to sit with the family, Dabir stood up to leave the room, right as Saheed had entered it.

As melo-dramatic as ever his red eyes scanned the room, "Are you all happy now?! She left! She's gone!"

Here we go again, Dabir thought to himself. How is this our fault?

"Saheed baby, don't worry, god has provided you with a better woman. A fruitful woman. That's why she is with child!" Mrs. Ayad brimmed, earning a glare from Sarai, Dabir and Mr. Ayad. "What? Are we to question his will?"

"How can you say this horrible thing he has done is God's will?! Does God permit adultery?!" Sarai questioned.

"How can you call this adultery?! He wasn't married to that girl. They merely were not a match. There's no harm. We all know she was never going to fit into this family."

Sarai scoffed, "Are you serious, Umi? How can you seriously take Saheed's side in this?"

"He is my son!" Mrs. Ayad snapped. "You will understand once you become a mother one day.

Saheed slid his back against the wall down until he was slumped on the ground. "Man, I don't even want that baby... What if she tries to get child support? Nah, I'm just going to act like I don't know her, I'm too young to be a dad."

"You are 30." Dabir spoke up for the first time in the conversation, he did not want to get involved but he also couldn't stand to hear Saheed make himself the victim in the situation. "The baby is the innocent one, not you."

Saheed quieted down. Ever since the other night when Saheed's life flashed before his eyes, he had been treading lightly around Dabir.

Thus came the end of the discussion. Life went on and it brought on the next day, and the next, and the one after that. Before they knew it, the situation with Gracie had come and gone, six months had gone by.

Chapter 15

Six months had gone by since the breakup, and life had been better than ever for Gracie Ademoye. She had spent the time working hard, reading, exercising, and spending time with true friends, her mom and her God. Gracie had even gone to therapy of her own to process through the nightmare relationship she was in.

It was a Saturday night and the girls were going out!

Leni would soon be starting her medical residency and beginning her career as Doctor. Gracie and Becca were bursting at the seams with pride and excitement for their friend, so it was with joy they planned a beautiful dinner at a luxurious, new restaurant.

Gracie had shimmied into her silk, emerald green dress and strappy heels. Her hair was in long, soft, body waves and she wore a poppy, red, lipstick with black winged eyeliner. When she was ready to go, she was sure to grab the YSL bag that Becca and her bought for Leni.

The restaurant was downtown and opened just a few weeks back. It served high-end Asian fusion and was split as a bar to offer a more 'lax' vibe. It was becoming a hub for all the well off 20-40 something's to go and enjoy time with their friends and for networking as well..

The trio got settled into their booth and took in the sights and sounds of all the people happily chatting and enjoying their food.

"Yall this is crazy! Oh my gosh, and thank you so much for this bag! It's so cute!" Leni gushed. She could be rough and tough around the edges, but at the end of the day she was a major softy. "Yall are the BEST friends I could ever have! Life has been amazing lately! I'm graduating from med school, Becca, you get married in two weeks. And Gracie...Well, Gracie is Gracie."

The three friends all burst out laughing, "Hey!"

"I'm just playin' girl, you have been killing it. I'm happy for you."

Gracie reached across the table and held the hands of both Becca and Leni. "I'm happy for us all. God has been so good."

"Yup! And it's going to be SO nice having a black woman as my OBGYN, we need more doctors who look like us." Becca grinned.

"Girl, I will not be your doctor, I don't want to be up in your hu-ha."

"After all these years waiting for you to finish this funky degree, you aren't going to be my doctor? So what did I spend all this time supporting you for?!"

"That's a question to ask yourself, Ms. Thing." Leni sipped her drink. "But I will not be looking between your legs."

"Ah, what?" Becca jokingly grabbed the bag that they had gifted Leni, "Come on Gracie, let's go."

Gracie snickered, "You two are too much! All this chatter, have you even looked at the menu yet?"

"Always worrying about food, I have no clue how you keep that little figure you got." Becca joked, causing Leni to laugh out loud.

"A girls gotta eat." Gracie shrugged.

"We sure do." Becca's eyes scanned the menu. "What sounds good to you?"

"Honestly, everything...I think I'm going to get the gochujang chicken with the–"

The waiter approached their table, interrupting the conversation. He placed a pale yellow drink in a champagne flute on the table in front of Gracie. "From the gentleman across the room."

"You can take it back to him, thank you." Gracie immediately responded, she did not even bother turning to see who it was, she was not interested in dating.

"Gracie!" Leni reached over and grabbed the drink. "Free is free, you don't gotta talk to him!"

Leni took a sip and practically spit it back out. "What is this?! The alcohol here is weak!"

"It's a nonalcoholic drink, ma'am. It's a citrus sparkling white tea."

Gracie's jaw dropped, "Leni! Why'd you spit it in? I love sparkling tea!"

"You didn't want it a second ago!"

"But I do now, I haven't had a sparkling tea since..." Gracie froze, she turned and began looking around the room. Other than her mom, the only person who knew her love of sparkling tea was Dabir. She looked around for a moment, but didn't see him, she sat back down.

"Who was it?"

"I don't know, I didn't see him."

"Who? You got a new boyfriend?"

"No, just a friend..." She turned her attention to the waiter, "Could I have another of those please?"

The pair went on to enjoy an absolutely exquisite meal. The drinks were good, food was better and the company was amazing. At the end of the night, Gracie was tearfully hugging her friends good bye. She enjoyed her time with them so deeply, it brought her to tears how much she loved her friends.

At the end of the night, Gracie stood near the valet kiosk, waiting for her ride to arrive. It was a chilly night, her hands held on to her biceps to keep warm as she waited.

A group of guys walked up a few feet to her left and chatted loudly amongst themselves. Gracie looked over and immediately caught one of the guys staring her down, when he saw her look at him he put a big, goofy smile on his face. Gracie rolled her eyes and got on her phone, pretending to be busy.

One by one, the men in the group walked over to Valet to get their cars brought up. The valet asked, "Last name and car make, model and year?" to each man, Gracie only passively listening in.

"Ayad, it's a 2022 Mercedes AMG SL."

Gracie's eyes shot up. She didn't know whether to leap into his arms or if she should run away. She gently placed a manicured hand on his arm, "Dabir?"

Every guy in the group turned and looked at Gracie. A smile spread on Dabir's face, he stepped closer to Gracie to greet her casually but the excitement took over and he leaned down and opened his arms for a hug.

Excitement took over Gracie as well, she wrapped her arms around his neck and hugged him tightly. As they embraced, he stood up straight causing Gracie's feet to clear off the floor. "Gracie."

"So it was you! You bought me that drink didn't you?"

"I did." He set her back on the ground, taking a step away. "I didn't want to disturb your time with your friends, I figured I would meet up with you after, but then you were gone."

"Gosh, I guess it's a good thing that my ride is so late." Gracie smiled up at Dabir. She felt her face heat up when she noticed his gaze on her. Gracie covered her smile with a hand and looked the other way "Stop."

"What?" Dabir knew exactly what she was talking about, she looked drop dead gorgeous and his eyes were fighting to stay on her.

Gracie playfully hit his arm. She pointed to the group of guys who were standing a few feet away, talking amongst themselves and staring at Gracie. "On a business meeting?"

"Those are my friends." Dabir turned back and saw that they all were watching Gracie intently.

"Are you going to introduce me?"

"Next time." Dabir nonchalantly moved to the right, blocking off his friend's view of Gracie. "You didn't answer my calls."

"Oh! I changed my number, I wanted a fresh start." Gracie quickly pulled her phone out of her YSL crossbody. "But gosh, it has been forever! Like...4 or five months since we've spoke?"

"Six, going seven."

They exchanged numbers and Gracie tucked her phone back in her purse. Just moments later, her ride pulled up. Dabir walked over and opened the door, just as he always did. When she sat down, he hesitated to close the door. Riskily, he said, "I want to take you out sometime."

A smile spread on Gracie's face, she sat up, "Okay! We can go to that Persian place you talked about."

"Gracie, no, listen to me. I'm saying I want to take you out. Not like before."

"Oh...Oh!" Gracie's face heated up. She initially thought that he wanted to take her out how they used to. She then realized that he was referring to a date. "Oh, um, okay. See you."

"Think about it."

Gracie looked the other way as he closed the door, her whole body felt on fire. She would be lying if she said that she never had a weird little crush on Dabir, but...that's her ex's brother! What would people say? Gracie used her hand to fan her face. Her mind ran wild with a host of thoughts:

Why does he have to be so cute?!

I want to say yes, but how will that make me look? Going between brothers?

Jesus, why didn't you let Dabir come first?! I could've saved so much time and tears!

I should say no, definitely say no

Gosh, but he's tall and handsome and thoughtful...WHY COULDN'T I HAVE MET HIM FIRST?!

Eenie, meenie, minnie, mo......

Chapter 16

It had been a few days since Gracie had seen Dabir at the restaurant, and she was still feeling conflicted.

After work, Gracie took a hot shower, put on her favorite body lotions, pajamas and ate leftovers. Her mom had gone on a trip back to Nigeria, so lately she had the whole house to herself.

Laying on the living room couch, Gracie toyed with her phone that she carried in her hands. She wanted to give Dabir a call, but was still so nervous. So far, she had spoken to Becca and Leni and they were in support. Her friends felt like there was no loyalty owed to Saheed, so it was best to explore the shared feelings with Dabir.

The situation was so weird that Gracie couldn't even bring herself to tell her mom.

Gracie sighed deeply. It was time to stop being so afraid.

She selected Dabir's name from her contact book....And after a few rings, she hung up. Her nerves got the best of her.

Her phone started to ring.

"Shoot! No!" Gracie panicked. She put a hand over her heart in a desperate attempt to calm down, with all the bravery she could muster, she answered his call. "Hello?"

"Hey."

"Hey."

"How are you?"

"I'm doing fine, just life and stuff you know?" Gracie nervously asked, she had never gotten that many butterflies from a guy before and it was making her cringe. "You?"

"I'm fine." His deep voice was smooth and strong like usual. "Just finishing up at work."

Gracie's eyes went to the clocks at 9pm. "That sounds about right."

Dabir lightly laughed. "I've been getting better about it."

"So..." Gracie fiddled with the hem of her pajama shorts. "How long has that...like...been on your mind?"

"What exactly?" As Dabir talked, he was packing up his stuff to go home. Gracie could hear the papers shuffling.

"You know.."

"You can be open. I've never given you reason to hide."

"Okay fine... Since when have you wanted to take me out like THAT? I mean, don't get me wrong...I kinda want to too. But aren't you, like, worried?"

"Worried about...?"

"Worried about what people will say!" She replied. "How will I look going from brother to brother?!"

He paused. "I suppose it didn't matter to me what others would say."

"What would your mom say? Or your dad?" Gracie huffed. "Gosh, what would Saheed have to say?!"

"Saheed doesn't get a say in any one's life other than his own. As for my father... I'm not sure, that's for time to tell. Either way, I am not concerned."

"What if he disowns you over something like this?"

"I'm not a child who needs to live in fear of being disowned." He responded. "Gracie, I've given them my entire life so far. I've given everything for the family name and business. This is the one thing I've loved to pursue on my own, does that make me wrong?"

Gracie's throat dried out. He said the word love.

Dabir continued talking, "I understand if you aren't comfortable with it, I don't want to make you uncomfortable, I won't do that to you. But I like you Gracie. If you like me too, I would like to take you out."

"How long have you liked me?"

"Long enough."

A smile spread on Gracie's face. She still felt nervous about the whole thing but was willing to try. After all, deep down she had feelings for him too. "Did you leave the office yet?"

"Not yet. I'm about to get in my car, do you need anything?"

"I want to see you." She squirmed in the couch, in utter disbelief that she was about to invite him over, her smittness was giving her the ick. "Can you come over for a little bit?"

"Of course. Do you need me to bring anything?"

"No, just come."

"Very well then. I will see you shortly."

After the phone call had ended, Gracie took off into the kitchen. She already knew that by this time Dabir had probably still had not eaten. Still in her matching pj set and bonnet. Gracie whipped up the tastiest and quickest pasta Alfredo dish she could.

At almost 10pm, she then took off her bonnet and got her long hair out of the rollers, leaving big body waves cascading down. Gracie then swiped on a clear coat of the first lip gloss she could find. Afterwards, she lit some candles to set a relaxed mood as well.

By the time that Dabir had arrived outside, Gracie had been scrambling all over the house for an hour straight.

Gracie opened the door after the first knock. The door opened wide, revealing Dabir who stood outside, towering over her. They shyly smiled at each other, and without a word went into a big hug. With her head on his chest, Gracie soaked in the security his strong arms provided, his signature cologne scent filling her nose.

When they had finally pulled out the hug, Gracie stepped back so that Dabir could come in. It had been six months since he was last there, but it felt like it was just yesterday. "Are you hungry?"

Dabir grinned.

"Of course you are." Gracie teased, walking into the kitchen to dish him out a plate of what she had cooked for him. She brought out the food and a large cup of ice water to the dining room table.

As he ate, Gracie sat on the chair next to him, sitting with her knees to her chest. They caught up on all that had been going on in each other's lives since the past six months.

Gracie had learned that Mr. Ayad had fully retired, appointing Dabir CEO of their business. With full control and stake, Dabir has been working on hiring the right people, to cut his work load down. Because of this, Dabir was no longer a billionaire's son, but he himself was now a billionaire.

Dabir had also gone against the family norm by buying his own house and moving out. It was expected for the eldest son to live, marry and raise kids in his parents house. But Dabir could no longer stay there. This happened after Mrs. Ayad had tried to move Alexis to the house unsuccessfully. It was unsuccessful because the night Alexis was supposed to come, Saheed went on a violent, drunken tirade with her. In the process, he earned himself a domestic violence charge for battery against a pregnant woman. That was Dabir's final straw. He bought himself a home and paid for an apartment for Sarai and two of her friends to move into as well.

Mr. Ayad's team of lawyers were working tirelessly to get the charges dropped and for Saheed to escape jail time.

Once fully caught up on the past, they moved into future plans. Gracie talked about wanting to move into remote teletherapy in the next few months or so, and all that her career had been. Gracie loved her work and her patients, but found herself wanting to scale back. She also talked about her best friend's recent accomplishments, including Leni becoming an OBGYN and Becca's upcoming wedding.

"So, are you... Free the 14th?" Gracie asked sweetly.

"I can always make myself available for you."

Gracie's face heated up, "Yeah right, even during your 100 hour work day?"

"I've put my work on pause for you in the past. I always will."

She couldn't hold back her smile. Dabir was always a sweetheart, but she would need time to get used to his romantic side. He was definitely sweeping Gracie off her feet.

"Anyways, the 14th is Becca's wedding date. I'll be busy since I'm in the bridal party, but I think it might be kinda fun to have you there as my date, maybe."

There was a twinkle in his pretty green eyes. "I'll be there."

"Okay, cool." Gracie smiled at Dabir, she was having a great time with him that night. But she couldn't ignore the fact that it was getting rather late. "Do you live close by? It's late, and I know you have work in the morning."

He looked at the time on his lustrous Rolex. "My house isn't that far from here. Maybe 45 minutes...?"

"45 minutes?! Oh my gosh, you might as well say an hour! Now I feel bad for asking you to come over. Are you going to be okay to drive? Are you sleepy?"

He stood up and began to put his suit jacket back on. Then stooped low to place a kiss on Gracie's temple. "I'm not a child. I'll be fine."

Gracie walked Dabir to the door, and stood on the front step to say goodbye. Dabir auto-started his car. "When can I see you next? I don't want to wait until the 14th."

"Hmm, maybe I can come visit you at your job this week?"

"You can visit me anytime you want to." He gently held her hand and kissed it. "But I'm talking about a real date. We can go anywhere you want to."

"Can you pick for me? I'm a little indecisive..."

"Okay. I will see you later this week."

After Dabir left, Gracie closed the door and leaned against it, both hands clutching her heart.. She was absolutely smitten. Gracie felt like a dork as a smile fought for its place on her face. She could not hold back the smile nor could she fight the feelings of their budding relationship being both wrong and right.

Chapter 17

The icky feeling Gracie felt when she thought about dating her ex's brother grew more and more. By afternoon of the following day, she had sent a text to Dabir canceling their date. It hurt her to do so, but it felt necessary, she couldn't shake the feeling.

A few days had passed and it was the 13th, the night before Becca's wedding. It had been a week full of activities and celebrations, Gracie stood outside the hotel where the bridesmaids had been staying, and took in the cold night air. The streets were bustling full of people, club goers and networking professionals alike. Big smiles were on every face all around, but inside Gracie felt uncharacteristically alone.

She leaned her back against the building behind her and unlocked her phone. Gracie stared at the two missed call notifications from Dabir. Desperately, she wanted to call him back and hear his deep yet calming voice. She wanted to look into his deep green eyes and see love looking back at her.

Gracie tucked her phone back into her purse right as a familiar arm touched her from behind.

"What are you doing out here?" Becca asked as she linked arms with Gracie. Becca wore a sash that said bride and wore a light blue mini dress. Her brown skin glowed from the love and excitement.

Gracie smiled sweetly to her friend, "I was just getting some air."

"What's on your mind G? It's him isn't it?"

"Oh gosh, Becca, no. This is your wedding weekend, we aren't talking about my guy drama."

"Oh yes we are." Becca protested, crossing her arms. "Girl, you weren't even this torn up over Saheed's little raggedy self and y'all were engaged. You obviously love Dabir, why won't you just let yourself be happy? I've never seen you this rattled by a man before, sis."

"This conversation can wait until after you come back from your honeymoon, happily and safely."

"No it can't, and it won't. Why won't you let yourself be happy?"

Gracie sighed and took a pause to collect her words. "What will people say?...They are brothers, Becca."

"Girl who cares?! If anyone talks, just know they are jealous because you pulled not one billionaire son but two." Becca shrugged, a mischievous smirk spreading on her face. "You know you're a savage right?"

"You play too much." Gracie playfully gave Becca a shrug.

Becca laced her hand with Gracie's, "Will you invite him to the wedding tomorrow? For me?"

"Becca..."

"For me!"

"Fine. But I doubt he will come, it's pretty last minute." Gracie let out a deep breath. "I'll ask."

"Thank you! Cause I want to see your future husband there with you!"

Gracie turned to Becca with a playful grin. "My girl is really getting married tomorrow. What am I going to do without you?"

The two hugged each other tightly. "What you're going to do is get married to Dabir and have you some babies so we can raise our kids together. That's the plan at least. Now it's either you text him or I will take your phone and do it myself!"

-

The next morning, all the bridesmaids held hands in a circle surrounding Becca in prayer. It was a tearful and raw experience, and they all cried tears of joy as they saw their dearest friend leave singlehood into a life of marital bliss.

The ceremony was outside, in a lush green field that was high and overlooking the city. The bridesmaids all stood alongside Becca in their figure hugging pastel pink dresses.

Gracie had been an emotional wreck all day, she felt like a proud parent as she watched Becca and Jorge exchange vows. Leni was also in her feelings as she threw back more champagne to numb the emotions. Leni looked over to Gracie, "Are we good? Why is this ******* me up like this?!"

"I don't know!" Gracie was exasperated, the emotional high was torture. As co-maid of honors, both Leni and Gracie shared the floor for the speech/toast. As the two spoke, a chronological slideshow played in the background, showing the trio in elementary, high school, college and into adulthood. No one in the room was safe from the free-falling tears.

Thankfully, soon came relief from the tears and heartache, and it came in the form of music and dancing.

As the night progressed and the music started, everyone was too busy dancing to the music to worry about their feelings. Gracie finally felt relief as she danced next to Leni with her eyes closed. Leni grabbed Gracie's hand and pulled her near. "3 o'clock!"

"Huh?"

"Girl, look at 3. O. CLOCK!"

Gracie looked around trying to find who it was, a small piece of her worried that Alexis had somehow crashed the wedding, coming to show off the massive baby bump that Saheed had happily given her. But no.

It was something that made Gracie's heart skip a beat, rather, it was someone.

All the way across the room, Dabir stood in his ash gray suit, looking around for Gracie. Gracie immediately noticed the lined up beard he had grown out. She swooned. He had no business being as handsome as he was.

Becca left her new husband's side to give Gracie a shove. "Is that who I think it is?"

Leni jumped in shock from Becca appearing behind them suddenly, "Girl shouldn't you be dancing with your husband?!"

"This is important! I already told Gracie, it's my dream!"

"What's your dream?!"

"What do you mean?! For her to marry Dabir and have kids at the same time that I do! I will go to the courts of heaven to plead with God about this it if I have to!"

Leni gave Becca a side eye, "And what about me? Where do I fit into this so-called little dream of yours?"

"...What do you mean? You're there! You're always part of our friendship trio."

"Uh huh, so only you two get to have kids together?"

"Len, God will do it for you at His own convenient time, you can't rush Him!" She teased, cracking up.

"Becca, God don't like ugly. I can't believe I was crying over you." Leni turned her attention to Gracie, "Girl, go get your man."

Butterflies fluttered in Gracie's stomach as she put one foot in front of the other towards Dabir. About half way over, he finally noticed her and their eyes locked. He stepped backwards and went outside the venue to the quiet hallway behind him. Gracie followed.

The two stood facing each other in silence, though she was nervous, she felt good to be next to him again.

"I'm sorry I'm late."

"That's okay, I'm surprised you came, it was kinda last minute." Gracie broke their eye contact. "Sorry for canceling on you last time, I—I just felt, well you know...It's—."

"It's okay. I'm not upset with you." He gently reached for and held one of her hands, he brought it up to his lips and gave it a kiss. "I'm not upset."

Gracie felt faint, she pulled her hand away from him and finally looked back up to him. "Dabir, what are we doing?"

"What do you mean?"

"I can't pretend I don't have strong feelings for you, but...you can't expect me to believe you really would be serious about a girl your brother used to date. I don't want to be some fling or some—."

"I love you."

The breath got caught in Gracie's throat. She took a step back but then two forward again.

Dabir, once again, held her hand. "You can question anything you want about me, but never my sincerity. I don't see you as Saheed's ex. To me, you are the woman I want to have a family with. I want to take care of you." Dabir let go of her hand. "I won't force you. It comes down to if this is something you want."

"What if it doesn't work out?"

"I'll make it work."

"Dabir, I'm not playing around with you. I don't want to get hurt again."

He bent down until they were eye level, and gently put his hands on her shoulders. "May God deal with me harshly if I hurt you."

"I'm serious."

"I am too."

Tears welled up in Gracie's big, brown eyes. Never had she seen a man look at her with such tenderness, love and genuineness. She covered her mouth and cried into her hands.

Dabir gently pulled her close and let her hand rest below his chest in an embrace. A few moments passed before he asked, "Is this what you want?"

Gracie did her best to wipe her tears away while hiding her face away from him, she knew her makeup was destroyed. "You wouldn't be ashamed to be with me?"

"I just told you I want to have kids with you."

"Guys have kids with girls they don't like all the time, that doesn't mean anything anymore." Gracie chuckled.

"I want to marry you." He truthfully but plainly responded. "I would ask you right here and now if it wasn't your friend's wedding...I heard that Americans don't like that."

She giggled, wiping more of her tears away, her face heating up. "You better not be playing me, Dabir. You know you could have literally any girl you want."

"Yes, and you're the only one I have eyes for."

"Well... Okay, I believe you. But stop staring at me."

"So beautiful." He held her face in his hands, but she swatted him away. "What?"

"I look like a mess right now, I've been crying for like 10 hours."

"You've always looked beautiful to me. From you eyes, to your smile..." His green eyes traveled down her feminine, shapely yet petite body.

Gracie playfully smacked his shoulder as her face heated up. She felt shy under his gaze yet wanted him to continue. "Eyes up here."

A bright white smile on his face. "No problem. My time will come soon."

Gracie smiled widely, it was new but it finally felt right. She knew it was worth it to take the leap of faith with Dabir. This time, she was the one who held his hands. "Come meet my friends."

Hand in hand, the new couple walked inside to the dance floor where Gracie's friends started, awestruck. Dabir was always the tallest person in the room and his striking Arab features always turned heads.

As they got near the dance floor, Becca ran as fast as her big wedding dress would allow her, and whispered something into the ear of the DJ.

Suddenly the fast, party songs slowed into sultry, romantic slow dance. Becca winked at Gracie before turning to her husband Jorge and wrapping her arms around him.

Couples began pairing up, slowly swaying. Dabir laughed, he could see what Becca had done. Dabir opened his arms to Gracie and she happily held on to his midsection. They swayed side-by-side as the world around them faded away.

She looked up and smiled at him, feeling more content and at peace than she ever had. He smiled back. Dabir was stern and stoic to the outside world, but to Gracie, he was nothing but cuddly and warm.

Chapter 18

----

2 Months Later

Gracie stood up from her office chair and stretched her arms over her head. She had seen clients back to back and was exhausted. It was now fall and the days were getting shorter. She put on her beige coat and slid her feet back into her crème colored, red bottom heels.

Gracie said good night to all of her coworkers before heading out the front door. Hakeem, her driver from time ago, was parked out front waiting for her. Dabir was never a fan of Gracie having to take Uber's and cab's all over, so he re-hired Hakeem for her.

As she walked to the car, her phone buzzed from an incoming call. She smiled as Dabir's name popped up on the screen. "Hey."

"Habibti, how are you?"

"I'm okay, just leaving work." Gracie sat in her seat and mouthed a thank you to Hakeem as he closed the door for her. "Are you at the office?"

"Yes."

"Well leave, it's already almost six."

"I need to finish reviewing a proposal that the marketing team has been working on." He replied, the sound of his typing audible in the background. "I want to see you, let me take you to dinner tonight."

"Sure! Where? I'm in the car with Hakeem right now, I can let him know."

"Don't worry, you can go home. I will meet you there."

"Are you sure you want to do all that driving?"

"I'm sure, I'm sure."

Gracie chuckled, "If you say so, see you soon, hubby."

When Gracie got home she had just enough time to refresh her makeup, hair and change into a date night look. She stepped into a red, off-shoulder long sleeve body con and paired it with a romantic red lipstick.

She didn't even know when Dabir had arrived, she just heard him downstairs talking with her mom.

"Why didn't he tell me he was here?" Gracie asked herself before hurrying downstairs. As soon as she was close to eye sight, the conversation between the two abruptly ended and they stared at Gracie. Gracie noticed a big smile on her mom's face and tears in her eyes, she was holding on to a big yellow folder in her hands. Gracie felt confused. "Mummy are you okay?!"

"I'm okay." She lightly laughed while wiping her eyes, she looked up at Dabir. "My God will bless you for me."

He smiled back at her, looking slightly choked up himself. Now Gracie was really freaked out, she never saw Dabir like that before. "Y'all what's going on?"

"Ah ah, we are just talking, what's the matter with you?" Gracie's mom laughed.

"Why y'all both crying?!"

"Who's crying?" She asked back, she looked at Dabir, "I'm not crying, were you crying?"

He shook his head no.

Gracie put a hand on her hip, "Fine. I'll find out eventually."

"You will." Dabir responded, before walking up to her and putting a hand on her low back. "Ready to go?"

And with that the pair were off. During the car ride to the restaurant, Gracie could feel something was off with Dabir. He was never known for being talkative by any means, but he was quieter than usual. It was like he was lost in thought.

The restaurant was a five-star steak house that was on the top floor of an expensive hotel. Inside, the lights were dim, with candles being one of the main sources of lighting.

They were led to a table in a private room, instead of the main dining floor where the other guests ate.

"Geeesh, This is beautiful." Gracie awed as she looked around the private room, she raised her eyebrow at Dabir when she looked at the menu prices. "You don't feel like this is a bit much? We aren't even celebrating anything."

"Life is for the living, habibti. Let me celebrate you every chance I get."

Gracie smiled sweetly and reached over the table to plant a kiss on his lips. Every time they spoke and met, she would see more and more of the depth of Dabir's love for her.

The dinner progressed beautifully. The food was amazing and the company shared was even better. The time for dessert had now come by and

Gracie was eating her chocolate cake as Dabir sat quietly across the table. "I don't know why you didn't order any, it's really good!"

"Not everyone likes sugar the way you do." Dabir rebuttaled, with a smirk. "I don't know anyone who likes sweets the way you do."

Gracie shrugged, taking another bite. "They' missing out."

A few more moments went by of her eating dessert in bliss. Meanwhile, Dabir's heart was beating quickly in his chest, he could no longer hold back what he wanted to do. "Baby, come here."

Gracie almost choked on the piece of cake that was in her mouth. Something about his tone and the way he said it had the room a few degrees hotter.

So she stood up and walked around the table towards him. He grabbed her hand and ushered her on to sitting on his lap. Gracie used her hand to cover the big smile on her face, that man had her shook. "What's gotten into you?"

"I want to give you something." He responded, his green eyes locked in hers.

From sitting on his lap, Gracie was able to smell that famous cologne on him that always drove her crazy. She wrapped her arms around his neck and gently ran her fingers over his styled hair, but lightly so as to not mess it up.

Dabir enjoyed her calming touch for a few quiet moments before he pulled out of it and reached for something in his jacket pocket.

It was a small black box.

Gracie's eyes widened.

He looked at her with sincerity, "You know where I am going with this."

"Dabir." Gracie put both hands up and covered her mouth, her heart beat quickly in her chest. As he opened the box, her jaw dropped.

The ring showed that Dabir truly did care and that he listened to her. Way back, when she was still with Saheed, during conversation Gracie had loosely mentioned to Dabir that her dream ring set had always been a yellow gold eternity band paired with a gold band. And that's exactly what was in front of her.

The 18k gold glistened, but not in comparison to the 10 dazzling carat's in the eternity band. Each beautiful diamond was perfectly set side-by-side all the way around.

He took the diamond band out of the box and slid it on to her ring finger, as he did so he asked. "Being my wife... is that what you want?"

"Oh, Dabir." Tears welled in her eyes, a smile she could not control was on her face. "Yes! Yes times 100!"

The two hugged tightly and followed it up with a fire-work producing, passionate kiss. Gracie felt overjoyed and it was Dabir's happiest moment as well. "We can do the wedding any way you like, whatever you want, whenever you want."

"I thought you were always the financially conservative one." Gracie teased, giving him another hug. "What's my budget?"

"I don't have a budget when it comes to my wife."

They shared another kiss, Gracie felt smitten by every word that would come out his mouth. "I want something small maybe...? I don't know, I spent so much time thinking the bigger the better, but I feel ready to be married now. Let's not wait."

"As you wish."

"Oh, we have to tell my mom! She's going to freak out!" Gracie excitedly got her phone to call her mom but Dabir stopped her.

"She already knows."

"How?... Is that what you two were talking about earlier?!"

He nodded yes, he held her hand and admired the way the ring looked on it.

"Just wait, she's going to start pestering you about a bride-price." Gracie laughed at the thought. Her mom had always looked forward to the day that she would get to exhort her future in-laws.

"The bride price has been settled."

Gracie gave him a look. "What do you mean? What did you give her?"

"Don't worry, just know that it has been settled and your mom supports our marriage."

"Come on, just tell me!"

"It's not good for a man to talk too much, you know how I feel about that."

"But I'm curious! Come on, we are getting married, you can't keep secrets." Gracie gave Dabir the most cutesy puppy dog eyes she could put on, hoping it would break him.

It worked.

"Okay, okay." He rubbed up and down her back. "I bought the house you guys have been renting, and put it under her name."

"What?!" Tears streamed down Gracie's face. "You did that for me mom?"

"She's my responsibility now, Habibti, don't make things like this a big deal." He wiped the tears on Gracie's face. "I don't want anything to trouble you."

She clung on to him, in a hug fueled by deep, sincere and mutual love for one another. When they pulled out of it, Gracie got the idea. "Hey, I think I want us to just go to the courthouse...Let's get married before we go to your family!"

"I'm not a child, it's not a concern of mine if they don't want us together. If we get married at the courthouse it will be because that is what we want, not because we are afraid of what anyone will say."

A smile crossed her face, she felt secure in the assurance he gave her. She knew that he was someone that she could truly trust with her forever.

So true to their word, they got married at a courthouse just one week later. It wasn't a secret, her best friends and mother witnessed...It was just the two of them. The world around didn't matter as they professed their love and vows before God and man.

As they got married, a hired crew of men moved all of Gracie's belongings into Dabir's house. The home they would now share together.

Chapter 19

After their nuptials, they spent a whole six weeks enjoying each other's company, each other's body and the beautiful decision they made together. It was finally time to reveal their marriage to the Ayad family. They had planned to have dinner with Mr. Ayad, Mrs. Ayad and Sarai.

Granted, Mr. Ayad already knew. Dabir met with him early in the week to let him know about the marriage, because Dabir wanted to mitigate any unnecessary drama that may unfold in front of the family. Mr. Ayad was at first confused, but it quickly began to make sense. By the end of the meeting, all he felt was heartbreak that he did not get to be there to witness the union.

Gracie and Dabir had just gotten out of the steamy shower together and Gracie walked into the bedroom to pick out the cream sweater dress that she wanted to wear for the night. She felt horribly queasy and took a seat on the edge of the bed. The nausea was on and off for a few days, but she couldn't figure out why.

After the wave of nausea passed, Grace got the dress and slid it over her freshly lotioned body, she noticed the buzzing of Dabir's phone in the background. "Baby! Someone's calling you."

"Who is it?" He asked from the bathroom, with a towel loosely wrapped around his waist, he steadily lined up his beard with trimmers.

Gracie walked over to the nightstand where his phone charged. She reached for the phone and then froze, a sinking feeling in her stomach.

The caller ID was as clear as day: BABA

Her heart beat sped up, her mind immediately going to the fact that Dabir's family still didn't know of their marriage. Gracie picked up and quickly walked it over to the bathroom.

Dabir was still focused on his beard, "Who is it?"

"It's—um, it's your dad, babe."

Dabir turned the trimmers off with a swift click. He was looking at himself in the mirror, letting out a sigh.

Just then the call ended. Almost instantly his dad was calling back. Dabir took the phone out of Gracie's hands and accepted the call. Right before Gracie's eyes, she saw the serious and stoic side of Dabir return as he held the phone up and said "Baba, ajb ealaa alhatif."

The phone was not on speaker phone but from where Gracie stood, she could hear the screaming and the crying. Dabir's face was straight, as he listened to his fathers panicked talking and the desperate crying of his step mom in the background.

Gracie felt anxiety course through her, she stood frozen in place, fearfully waiting for the call to end and to find out what happened.

Minutes went by before Dabir placed the phone down and used his both hands to grip the counter top. He tilted his head down and closed his eyes, a slew of different emotions making their way through his heart and mind.

Gracie put one hand on his forearm and the other on his back. "Baby what is it? What happened?"

Dabir's took deep, staggered breaths. He wanted to open his mouth to talk but couldn't bring the words to his mouth. Painful tears rose to his eyes and he fought like hell to suppress them back down.

"Please, you're scaring me. What happened? Is everything okay?"

"I–" Dabir cleared his voice to prevent it from cracking. "It's Saheed. He's–."

Gracie took a step back in shock, she held onto the counter to brace herself. It was extremely uncomfortable for Gracie to talk about Saheed to Dabir. "What happened to him?"

"Don't worry. I will go handle it."

"Are we still going to dinner tonight?"

"I'm sorry, Habibti. Tonight is no longer a good night for that." Dabir smoothed her hair out her face and kissed her. "Come, I will drop you off with your mother before I go."

Chapter 20

The few weeks of peace were nice while they lasted, but as Dabir drove, he found himself tense and on edge. He was driving to the hospital to see his estranged brother for the first time in months.

Mr. Ayad confessed that he let it slip to Mrs. Ayad about Dabir and Gracie's marriage. Mrs. Ayad immediately went to Saheed, and it went downhill from there. Saheed had drunk and pill-popped himself to a stupor. A night club attendant found him unresponsive and slumped against the floor with his wallet emptied out.

When Dabir got to the hospital, he rushed inside to see his family. In the lobby, he was immediately confronted by an inconsolable Mrs. Ayad. She was filled with disgust and hatred. With red eyes and black streaks of eyeliner running down her face she stood up and marched right to Dabir, slamming both hands against his chest. In hysterics, she yelled, "You did this! You did this to him! How could you do this to your own brother?"

Dabir did not respond. He let out a deep breath as she continued to fling out all sorts of curses at him. Mr. Ayad wrapped both arms around Mrs. Ayad and squeezed tightly, "YA! What's gotten into you, woman? Conduct yourself!"

"It's that EVIL son of yours who caused this! You took his true love away from him!" She screamed. Two of the head-housegirls quickly came to Mrs. Ayad's side and ushered her into the hallway for comfort.

Mr. Ayad ran a hand through his sparse hair as he watched his wife walk away. There were tears in Mr. Ayad's eyes as well. "My son, don't mind her."

"It's okay." Dabir responded calmly. "How is he?"

"He...He will live, but...He will need dialysis, his kidneys have failed."

Dabir let out a big breath. It felt like he got punched in the gut. Though he didn't speak to Saheed, he still cared. "Is he awake?"

"Room 306B. Do you want to go see him?"

"Yes. I will go alone."

As he stepped forward, Mr. Ayad caught a glimpse of the yellow gold wedding band on Dabir's finger. "Ya... How is she?"

Dabir caught his dad's glance at the ring. "She's fine. She's at home."

"Okay— My son, I know it might feel odd, but please, reconsider moving back in with us. You are the heir to our throne, it's not right for you to be far."

"Baba, it's not the time for this."

"Yes! It is! Yasmeen might be upset, but she won't stay upset forever. It would be an honor for me to welcome you and your wife back."

Dabir's eyes narrowed, he wondered if his father could even hear how silly he sounded. "How do you expect me to subject my wife to that?"

"To what? I loved her like I love Sarai!" He huffed, offended that Dabir would question him. "It was our Imam who told me that Gracie was destined to be an Ayad, that's why I celebrated when you told me of your marriage with. So how can you now question what she would be subjected to? Am I that horrible of a father to you?"

"Baba." Dabir let out a breath. "I won't move my wife into the same home Saheed and your wife are in. I won't be discussing this matter further."

And with that, Dabir turned and walked off to Room 306B. Despite their brotherhood being estranged, Dabir still cared. He lightly knocked on the door before opening it up and taking a step in. A nurse was finishing up a lab draw on him, she shyly excused herself as Dabir and Saheed silently looked at each other.

Saheed laid his head back on his pillow, staring up at the ceiling. "Surprised to see you here."

"I imagined." Dabir replied. He sat down across the room, and put his elbows to his knees. "We need to talk."

"Don't bother. I already know about you and Gracie." He weakly looked over to Dabir. "I don't care anymore... If Baba won't put me on an allowance, Umi will. Especially now that I've... you know."

"Now that you've almost killed yourself? Saheed, listen to me and listen carefully." Dabir was fired-up, he absentmindedly switched from speaking in English to Arabic. "It's time to grow up and take responsibility for your actions. It's time that you find your own way in this life. After my mother died, Baba immediately married your mom and not long after came you and Sarai. Despite the pain I felt, I immediately loved you and Sarai, aqsam biallah. I've never held ill-will against you...I have no idea where your hatred for me has come from, I don't know where it started but you are allowing it to ruin your life. If you never want to speak to me again, that's fine, but for your own sake Saheed, enough is enough...As for Gracie, I don't owe you an explanation, but because I want you to have a peace of mind, know that we didn't become romantic until months after you two were over. We were just friends prior to that point and now we are married, we will be having children. That's the last I'll speak about it."

Saheed had his head turned to the opposite side of the room that Dabir was in. There was a cascade of fiery tears streaming down his face. He cried silently for a few moments, wanting to speak but being unable.

"I'm not your enemy, Shaqiq."

"So what–You expect me to just go get a job or-or go to school or something? Hm? Hm?"

"If you get a business plan, I am happy to help fund–"

"You don't get it do you? I'm NOT you. I will NEVER be you. I just want to live my life, I wish you and Baba would stop bugging me about a job!"

"Alright, okay. I understand." Dabir calmly responded, looking at the spike on Saheed's heart rate monitor.

"I don't want to work, man... I just want to...Be free! You know?! You don't ever get tired of being an Ayad? I just need to be free. I can't ******* breathe sometimes."

At that moment, the wires connected to Dabir. Saheed's behavior made perfect sense. The pressures of being the perfect son was at the root of Saheed's problems. Between the angst from his Baba and the vindictive manipulation from his Umi, Saheed was finding his escape in drinking, drugs and girls.

Dabir's heart broke at the realization. Saheed turned to his vices for escape, but Dabir knew he was no better. The only difference is he turned to workaholism to keep him away from the dysfunction. "I understand." Dabir breathed.

"No you don't! You've always been the perfect one. Baba's favorite."

"It was never a matter of favoritism. My performance kept him happy and made him look good." Dabir replied, all in one breath. He locked eyes with his little brother, "You found your escape in parties, I found mine in work. I understand. We are both too old to worry about being a favorite."

"Really...Oh." Saheed weakly sat up. "Well now what? Should I just–I don't know, are you telling me to just do what I want?"

"What is it that you want?"

"I guess... I always liked the idea of having a clothing line or something." Saheed quietly responded, he felt silly to talk about it, he didn't want Dabir to shoot him down. "But probably not though."

"If that's what you want to do, then do it."

"Nah, you probably think it's stupid."

"Saheed, if that's what you want to do, then do it." He firmly re-assured, "It doesn't matter what me or anyone else thinks."

Saheed perked up, for the first time in years he felt hope. "Alright...I've never worked before, what do I need to do first?"

"Before anything, you need to get your health in order. There's no purpose in having a legacy if you are going to then die an untimely preventable death. You should strongly consider rehab. After you are cleared, I can connect you to my friend who is a business consultant, Daud."

"Oh, yeah, right...Rehab, I probably should, huh? Well, thanks anyways man. I'm gonna do what we talked about... I'll get my **** together, forreal this time."

"Okay." Dabir stood to his feet. "Okay then, I'll be off."

"No problem, do your thing. Tell Gracie I said hi." Saheed replied, Dabir immediately shot him a warning look. It did not matter if the pair were reconciled, Gracie would forever be Dabir's weak point. He didn't like Saheed even saying her name. Saheed could sense the energy shift on Dabir and put his hands up in surrender. "I'm not trolling! Trying to be nice, but fine, I get it. Conversation for another day...or year."

Dabir let out the breath he was holding and gave Saheed a slight nod before turning to leave. On his way out he ran into his father who was practically pressed against the door trying to overhear what Dabir and Saheed had been talking about. Dabir quickly shut the door behind him before Saheed saw and got worked up. "Why?"

Baba was ashamed but his pride wouldn't let him say so. "I was just leaning here, my back is stiff from all the sitting."

"Then you should go and ask the nurses for a Tylenol." Dabir coldly responded, he was getting sick of the familial charades. "I will see you later."

"You're going already? Sit and talk with me first, my son."

Dabir's focused was pulled away, there were multiple missed calls from Gracie that he did not notice until that moment. His heartbeat picked up and he immediately felt flush. Without saying another word, he began to go straight to the car park to find his car. Gracie answered right as he got to the car door. "My love, what is it?"

There was chatter in the background, "Oh it's nothing serious, baby, I just wanted to let you know that Becca and Leni came over for an impromptu girls night."

His shoulders fell as he leaned his body against the car. "Gracie, don't call me that many times if it's not an emergency."

"Sorry, I just didn't want you to be surprised when you got here!."

"I know, it's fine, just for next time, okay? I'll be home soon."

"Bye hubs!" Gracie then ended the call.

Dabir stood in the cement, silent parking garage and felt the weight of the world on him. He got into his car and threw the car keys to the passenger side. He was more on edge than he ever had been. Before he knew it, Dabir found himself in a full-blown breakdown.

He cried, and cried and cried some more.

It was his first time crying since his mother died. Between the reconciliation with his brother, the pressure from his father and his intense protective instinct over Gracie... Dabir was emotionally spent.

Chapter 21

Gracie was having a blast with her two best friends, as they ate take-out and watched reality tv. Gracie desperately craved Indian take-out and loved every bite of it. That is...until it stopped loving her back.

As a strong wave of nausea hit Gracie, she quickly put her plate on the side table and made a bee-line for the bathroom. The food all came up the same direction it went down, and Gracie felt devastated because of it.

After washing her face and brushing her teeth, Gracie went back out to the living room where her friends looked at her with concern. Becca tilted her head. "Girl, you good?"

"I hope so." Gracie plopped down on the couch and laid out, she still felt sick. "I don't know what that was, but I'm mad I didn't get to finish my food. I have no idea why I've felt so sick lately, this is getting ridiculous."

Leni walked over and felt Gracie's forehead. "How long have you felt this way?"

"It's just been a few days."

"And when was your last period?"

Gracie glared at Leni, "Ha-ha, very funny."

"I'm serious girl! The way you have been bussin' down with Dabir, you're probably pregnant."

"My period isn't late. Here, we can look at my period app." Gracie unlocked her phone and went to the app she used to track her cycles.

8 Days Late

Gracie became speechless while Leni smiled widely at Becca and crossed her arms over her chest. "Gracie, you're pregnant."

"You don't know that." Gracie defended. She always wanted to be a mom, but she couldn't help but feel overwhelmed.

"Uh, remember me?" Leni wave. "Dr. Leni Carmichael? Board-certified OBGYN? Gave you a PAP smear like a month ago?! I'm not God...But I'm willing to put money on this."

Becca clasped her hands together as her eyes watered from excitement. "Oh my gosh! You're going to be a mommy!"

"Becca! I have to take a test first. Let's go to the drug store." Gracie quickly sat up, then quickly laid back down once she felt her nausea intensify from the movement. "Tomorrow...tomorrow we will go to the drug store, today I sleep."

"You best believe we will be holding you to that" Becca laid on the couch next to Gracie and hugged her. "You don't seem excited, what's wrong mama?"

Gracie sighed, no matter how hard she tried, her friends could always read her. "I really want a baby, yall, I do. I guess I'm just scared? With this whole endometriosis nonsense, I was always told it would be hard to get pregnant and hard to keep a pregnancy. I want a baby but it feels too good to be true, I'm not going to let myself get too excited until I know it's for sure."

Leni sat down by Gracie's feet. "No ma'am, that's what we aren't about to do tonight. There's no need to doubt what God's already done. How about this.. I can open up some time tomorrow, why don't you and Dabir stop by? I can have some labs run and we can see what's going on."

"Ugh, you two are the best." Gracie's eyes were watery. She sat up slowly and pulled both Leni and Becca into a group hug. As they pulled out the hug, the sound of the garage opening was heard. "Oh gosh, sound like Dabir's home."

"Let me know what time tomorrow works for you two, I will make it work." Leni gave Gracie another squeeze, before turning to Becca. "Alright Miss. Thing, let's go."

"Go? Go where? I need to take care of my Gracie-girl and make sure she is okay!"

"Girl what are you talking about, her husband is here." Leni replied. "And YOUR husband is probably at home waiting for you."

"Well he can wait."

"I can't! See this is why I never ride with your ***, it's always pulling teeth to get you to leave at a reasonable time!"

Dabir then walked in from the garage, his face looked flushed, almost as if he had just finished running a marathon. He politely smiled at Becca and Leni, "How are you all doing?"

"We good! We were just about to get gone." Leni nudged Becca. "Right?"

"Yeah, right." Becca said defeatedly, getting up from the couch and grabbing her purse.

"Don't let me end your fun early. I will be upstairs."

"Oh it's not you, it's getting late. You two have a good night." Leni hugged Gracie and then Dabir.

When Becca gave her goodbye hug to Dabir, at the last moment she whispered. "You take care of her, she's got precious cargo."

Dabir was confused to say the least. He was also exhausted, too exhausted to try and make sense of it. He liked Gracie's friends but often did not understand what they were talking about.

Gracie walked her friends outside and ended up getting into another conversation with them while they sat in the car letting it warm up. A few minutes of the chatting went by before Dabir came out the front door. "Gracie, yalla."

"Okay I'm coming!" Gracie blew both Leni and Becca a kiss before hurrying off back inside the house.

As soon as she got inside, Dabir closed the door behind her and locked the door. He turned on the home alarm system. Gracie reached her arms up for a hug, he bent down—allowing Gracie to wrap her arms around his neck. "How did it go with your family? Is everything alright?"

"Everything is fine."

Gracie took a step back out the hug, "Thank God, I was worried that something bad had happened to someone. Did you eat dinner while you were out? I have some lef–"

"It's okay, I'm not hungry. I'm going to go to bed." Dabir pulled his shirt off and began walking up the stairs.

Gracie followed behind, she was mentally debating on whether she wanted to bring up the possible pregnancy or not. A smile spread across Gracie's face. "There's something I want to talk to you about."

"Can we talk about it in the morning?" Dabir asked as he pulled his pants off and sat on the edge of the bed. He began working on the clasp to remove his Rolex wrist watch.

"Why don't you feel like talking? Is something wrong?"

"I am tired, Habibti."

Gracie sat up against the headboard and crossed her arms over her chest. "Too tired to talk to your wife? I don't treat you like that when I'm tired."

"How am I treating you?"

"Coldly! Like you don't care. What if what I had to tell you was important? You're just assuming that it's not."

"That's not the case."

"What's the case then? You're usually so happy to see me."

"I'm always happy to see you. It was a long day and I just don't feel like talking right now."

"Well yeah, it's you, you're never much of a talker. All you have to do is listen."

"My love, I just told you that I want to sleep. Please. There's a lot on my mind."

"Then tell me what's on your mind, why do you like to bottle things up so much?"

Dabir let out a deep breath and put his head in his hands. He deeply loved Gracie and loved being married to her, but in that moment, he desperately needed peace and quiet. He had been on his own for so long, he didn't know how to deal with his need for space when his wife needed attention at the same time. Under his breath he said, "Allah Arhameh" (Translation: God have mercy)

"Fine, you don't want to talk to me, don't talk to me. Good night."

"Thank you. Good night." Dabir laid his head back and closed his eyes. Foolishly, he thought Gracie was being understanding and agreeable when she said goodnight. Little did he know, hormonal fury was on its way.

"You really don't care about me do you?! What did I do to get this mood from you today?"

Dabir's heart raced as his eyes shot back open. He was now losing his grasp on his more collected affect. Just like Gracie, his anger was starting to kick in. "Gracie, stop this. Say what you want to say."

"Oh you want me to just say it?!"

"Yes."

Gracie rolled her eyes and got into her side of the bed, wrapping herself in the covers, her back to Dabir. "Forget it."

Dabir sat up in bed, looking at his upset wife. He let out a big breath and then moved over to where Gracie was. He hugged her while in big spoon. "I'm sorry. It was not my intention to hurt you.

Silence.

"You have my full attention. Tell me what is on your mind."

Silence.

"Is it not you I'm talking to?" Dabir teasingly asked, before plotting a kiss on Gracies shoulder. A smile spread on his face. "You're ignoring your husband? Your darling husband?"

Gracie did everything to keep from laughing, she hid her smile.It was impossible for the two to stay upset for very long.

"You need to hear I'm sorry in a different language maybe? Okay fine." Dabir kissed Gracie's cheek this time. "Habib albi, ya hayati...Ana asef." (Translation: Love of my heart, my life. I'm sorry)

And more silence...

"Tamam, let's reason with each other. Name whatever you want, it's done." (Translation: Fine)

Gracie rolled over to face him, a big, bright, mischievous smile on her face. "What's my budget?"

"I don't have a budget for my wife."

"Okay fine, you've successfully bought my forgiveness." Gracie joked, she scooted closer to her husband and the two shared a kiss. "I'll tell you what I want you to buy for me tomorrow. Let's go to dinner together."

"We will do that. Before you forget, what is it you had to say?"

Gracie smiled but shook her head no. She suddenly wanted to wait until it was on paper and confirmed, the last thing she wanted to do was get Dabir's hopes up and back down again.

The two got into their typical cuddling positions and Gracie shortly after drifted off into sleep. Dabir, though tired, was kept awake with his mind back on Saheed.

Chapter 22

"You don't think this is a bit much?" Gracie asked, looking down at the hospital gown. "I thought I was just going to pee on a stick or something."

"No I don't think it's a bit much! I wanna see what's going on inside of you while we wait for the HCG lab results."

"Oh, yeah! About that, you didn't tell me I was getting my blood drawn! Seriously uncool, I hate needles and you know it!

"Girl if you don't lay back and shut it up, I'm gonna do more labs." Leni demeaned. Her setup was orderly and sterile. Leni switched the lights off and brought out the ultrasound gel. "Move your gown up."

Gracie moved her hospital gown, exposing her flat stomach. She shook her head as the cold, ultrasound gel spread over her lower abdomen. "If anyone tells me that they are getting medical care from a best friend, I'll be sure to discourage them. Never again."

"Shh!"

"Are you usually this cold to your patients? I'm going to file a complaint!" Gracie huffed, she waited for Leni to respond but Leni's eyes were laser-focused on the screen. Her face was emotionless as she viewed the ultrasound screen intently.

"Huh. Strange." Leni said under her breath, moving the ultrasound wand and applying a slight more amount of pressure.

"What's strange?"

"Shh."

"Leni, what's strange?"

Leni put the wand she was using down and picked up a different attachment. It was long, and less thick than the previous one. Leni opened a drawer and pulled out a condom, she swiftly rolled it down the long attachment.

"You're joking." Gracie flatly stated. "You aren't putting that in my body."

"Yes ma'am, I am."

Gracie scoffed, "You won't ever see me in this building again."

"Girl, will you stop complaining? Even my 16-year old patients don't give me this hard a time!" Leni huffed. "Look, the images from your ultrasound were...inconclusive. I want to go in transvaginally, as it will give me a clearer view of what I'm trying to see."

"Okay....Well, can't we wait for the blood results? I don't want to get prodded around if I don't need to be. Is there something weird going on? I mean, there is either a baby there or there isn't, right?"

"This actually isn't a matter of pregnancy. It's the shape of your uterus, I think I know what's going on but I want to be sure. I'm your doctor, but I'm your friend first, let me work."

Gracie laid her head back on the exam table. "Never again" she thought to herself, as the ultrasound wand entered her body.

It was a few minutes of Leni silent working before the exam room door opened. There was thankfully a curtain at the entrance, so the tech was unable to see the exposed Gracie.

"Doctor, we just got the labs back. HCG came in at 3,432 mIU/mL."

"Thank you, please have the results added to the AVS."

As soon as the sound of the door closing was audible, Gracie sat up again. 'Is that good."

"That's great. You're definitely pregnant." Leni responded with a bittersweet facial expression, she laid the ultrasound wand down and removed her gloves. "Congratulations, girl. You're going to be a momma."

Gracie felt a slurry of emotions, but overall a sense of joy. "Were you able to see the baby?"

"It's a little bit too early, likely by next week we could see it. Your HCG levels certainly confirm a pregnancy There are few things we will need to go over."

"Oh, okay, what? What is it?"

"Gracie, you have a...well, clinically it's called a bicornuate uterus, in simpler terms your uterus is literally shaped like a heart–" Leni pointed to the ultrasound screen and used her finger to trace the black and white image. "This affects about 4 in 1,000 women."

"Oh, it's kind of cute."

"While I agree, you should know that women with heart shaped uteruses are at a higher risk of pregnancy complications. The shape makes things a little more cramped for the baby, so it's quite likely that you will need a C-section."

"C-section? Oh geez, I don't want to have a C-section!"

"Hey, hey.It's going to be fine. You already know you have access to the best medical treatment money can allow, don't stress, okay? I'll be here, my team will be here and you are going to have a healthy baby okay?"

"Okay." She took in a deep breath to keep from having an anxiety flare.

"You're alright girl. All you need is a bit more caution, feel me? Take it easy and limit stress. Here are foods you will need to avoid, and I'm sending you home with a prescription to a high-quality prenatal and Pyridoxine for nausea." Leni handed Gracie a packet that was filled with all the do's and don'ts.

After Gracie got dressed, she met Leni back out front. Leni gave Gracie a tight hug and a kiss on the cheek. "That baby is too blessed to have you and Dabir as parents. We are going to throw the biggest baby shower for you girl."

"You think we are still friends after how you did me in there?" The two laughed, Leni gave her a light, playful shove. "That was not proper bedside manner."

"Bedside manners are for patients, you are my homegirl, you get the pre-white coat Leni."

"Uh huh, let's see how long that lasts for you." Gracie gave Leni another hug. "But thank you for today, sis. I will FaceTime you and Becca sometime tonight or tomorrow."

"You better. Get home safe, Baby Mama."

A few hours later, Gracie was stepping out of the shower to get ready for her dinner date. She stared at her stomach in the mirror and tried to visualize herself with a large, baby bump. Her hand rubbed her stomach gently, as a smile found its way on her face. All afternoon Gracie felt terribly nervous about the possibility of miscarrying, but in that moment she felt grateful.

Gracie settled on a simple, burnt-orange, sweater dress and light makeup. She chose a cream colored cross-body bag to pair with it. Neatly, she tucked in the printed test results, she wanted to surprise Dabir with the news over dinner.

After getting ready to go, Gracie went downstairs and waited for Dabir to come home so they could go. While she waited, she joined the WhatToExpect forums and tried to read as much as she could about pregnancy with a bicornuate uterus.

So focused on what she was doing, Gracie did not notice when the garage door began to open and Dabir came into their abode. She flinched when she saw him across the room and held her chest from the fright. "Gosh, you scared me!"

"How can you be afraid when you are in your husband's house?" Dabir teased before walking over to Gracie and planting a kiss on her lips. "You look beautiful, habibti."

"Thank you, hubby, are you ready to go?"

"Oh, that's right. Yes, yes, I'm ready. Let's go."

And with that, the pair were on their way. Gracie was craving some of the Arab dishes she used to enjoy when living at the Ayad Mansion. Because of this, Ayad took Gracie to a little, mom n' pop restaurant about 30 minutes outside of town.

It was nothing worth looking at, but inside it smelled and looked like a snug, traditional Arab living room. Dabir's eyes lit up at the same. It felt like home.

When it was time to order, Gracie let Dabir pick for her. Partially because he had better recommendations and Gracie knew that he was always itching for the opportunity to speak in his native tongue.

Dabir reached across the table and held both of Gracie's hands, he brought them up and over to his lips, decorating her hands with kisses. Gracie's face heated up, he always had a way of making her blush like a schoolgirl with her first crush.

They talked about Dabir's work day and all that happened. He was working on opening up a satellite office in Abu Dhabi and the process for permitting and licensing was proving to be more time consuming than Dabir had imagined. Being that they were indigenous to Abu Dhabi, Dabir and Mr. Ayad always had the vision to see AES in the home land, and now that dream was in the process of coming true.

"How much longer until you resume work? I want to take you there so you can see my country."

"Yeah, about that..." Gracie slowly pulled her hands back. "There is something I need to talk to you about."

"What is it?" There was a slight look of concern in Dabir's eyes.

"I don't think I want to work anymore, I don't even think I'm supposed to work, well, at least for now. Maybe just being a tele-therapist?--I don't know exactly, I obviously haven't thought this through very much..."

"Tell me what is going on."

"Okay, well, I think I'm—no, today I found out that I'm pregnant." Gracie reached into her bag and pulled out the lab results to give to Dabir.

Dabir's stunning green eyes scanned the lab results, he looked at Gracie with a deep, unwavering eye-contact. "You're being serious?"

"Yes. I got the lab results from Leni's office today."

"I know how Leni and Becca like to get a reaction from me."

"Honey, this is serious. I'm really pregnant."

A big smile spread on Dabir's face, his straight white teeth glistened. "Alhamdulilah. This is—" (Translation: Praise God).

"Before you get excited or anything like that...Leni did find that my uterus is really cute but not very hospitable for a baby. It's going to be higher risk. I'm going to do everything on my end to ensure that this works out for us, but I only have so much control. Let's just see how it goes to avoid getting hurt."

"No, my love, don't see it that way. This is reason to celebrate and appreciate their life."

"Of course, but what if we never get to hold this baby in our arms?" Gracie asked, feeling the worry rising to the surface yet again.

"We will get to hold them, by God's grace." He kissed her hand. "Whether or not we hold them in our arms, they will also be our oldest child so we must love them unconditionally for as long as we have them."

Tears welled in Gracie's eyes, she felt overwhelmed with gratitude to God for being married to a man like Dabir and now to be carrying his baby. From the time that Dabir got married to Gracie he felt his life became complete, but news of the pregnancy was an immense added bonus. After the tragedy of his brother's health decline, the chance at fatherhood rejuvenated Dabir. He was never the type to be extravagant in behavior or animated, but on the inside, his spirit was experiencing joy unspeakable.